## "I MUST THANK YOU
## FOR COMING TO MY AID,"

Sylvia managed to say. Bennett's arms were about
her, and she was aware of a strange, warm feeling
deep within her, something quite unknown to her,
but something quite wonderful.

"You know you can command me at any time, my
lady." Then, with an effort, as he remembered who
this lady was, Bennett stepped backward and shook
his head, as if to free himself from the emotion which
had nearly overpowered him. It had felt so natural to
hold her; in another instant, he would have kissed her.
How had this situation come about?

He bowed over the hand she had extended, brushing
it with his lips, steeling himself against a wish to make
the caress a more ardent one. . . .

*Diamond Books by Monette Cummings*

A HUSBAND FOR HOLLY
SCARLET LADY
A KISS FOR CAROLINE
THE WICKED STEPDAUGHTER

# The Wicked Stepdaughter

## Monette Cummings

DIAMOND BOOKS, NEW YORK

THE WICKED STEPDAUGHTER

A Diamond Book / published by arrangement with
the author

PRINTING HISTORY
Diamond edition / January 1992

ISBN: 1-55773-651-0

Diamond Books are published by The Berkley Publishing Group,
200 Madison Avenue, New York, New York 10016.
The name "DIAMOND" and its logo are trademarks
belonging to Charter Communications, Inc.

PRINTED IN THE UNITED STATES OF AMERICA

10  9  8  7  6  5  4  3  2  1

# CHAPTER
## ❧ 1 ❧

The dark-haired young lady paced angrily back and forth, pausing from time to time to scowl down at the other occupant of the drawing room, who was only slightly older than herself. "I cannot believe you would consider doing such a thing." *Even you*, her tone seemed to say.

"Nonetheless, I am considering it." Although the older lady had sometimes found the folds of the heavy black cloth of mourning smothering, she had worn the mourning dresses dutifully. Now the time had come for her to put them aside. "There is no reason why I should not do so."

"But Papa—"

A faint flush tinging her pale cheeks at this criticism from her stepdaughter—not that she had expected anything else—Sylvia, Countess of Harmin, smoothed back

*1*

an errant lock of fair hair and fastened it in place. These unpleasant scenes had always disturbed her and she avoided them whenever possible. Charlotte appeared to know her stepmother's aversion to quarreling quite well and, during the years, had often used it to her advantage.

On this occasion, however, Sylvia said firmly, "Your papa has been dead these eighteen months. I do not believe he would wish that I should wear mourning for him forever."

"The black you wore was nothing but a farce, to deceive everyone. But I was never fooled—*I* do not believe you have mourned him for an instant."

There was spite in Lady Charlotte's tones, spite her stepmother had known quite well the girl would show to any decision the older lady had made. Sylvia looked at the girl for a moment, thought of replying, then shrugged. It would be impossible, she knew, to say anything that would change her stepdaughter's opinion.

Sylvia had become fond of her husband despite the difference in their ages, but she knew it would be useless for her to say so. Charlotte would not believe her—would not wish to believe her.

Instead of attempting to argue, the countess said, "I know quite well what you think, for you have told me often enough. And it is true that your father's and mine was scarcely a love match—on either side. Still, I have been wearing mourning for him for a year and a half. I intend to do so no longer."

Charlotte sniffed.

Sylvia continued, "Besides, we now have the matter of your come-out to consider. I believe that even you will own that I can scarcely present you to the *ton* while I am still in black."

It was clear from her expression that Charlotte had not considered this. She did so now for several moments. "But why could not my Aunt Diantha take care of—"

The young countess laughed.

"Your aunt Diantha has been a recluse for the past twenty years, and would scarcely be willing or able to undertake such an arduous task as the handling your presentation."

The girl began a further protest, but her stepmother continued, "Remember, although all of his unentailed property comes to you, he left me the control of your fortune until you come of age—or marry."

"Then I shall marry as quickly as possible!"

"But even then, you will receive your money only if I approve the husband of your choice."

Charlotte's scowl deepened.

"And you never will approve, will you?" the girl said angrily. "No matter whom I might choose!"

She flung out of the room, slamming the door behind her. Sylvia looked after her, sighing. Seventeen was such a difficult age, and she probably shouldn't have reminded the girl how much she was still in control.

And yet, as she recalled, it had not been like that for her; there had been no feeling that she was being deprived of her rights. She had been just seventeen, still enjoying the minor triumphs of her first London Season, when she had permitted herself to be convinced that she should marry Martin and that Sylvia and his daughter would become good friends. It had been a rude shock to the couple when he brought her home and proclaimed, "This is your new mama."

The eleven-year-old Charlotte had flown at her like a small, bad-tempered child, pounding at her with both fists.

"You are not my mama," she cried. "You will never be my mama. I want you to go away. Leave us alone!" Then she dashed from the room. They could hear her angry shrieks as she ran up the stairs to the nursery on the top floor, although she had long since declared herself too old to remain there and had installed herself in her late mother's bedchamber, next to her father's.

The earl had been completely bewildered by Charlotte's outburst. He was not the sort of man who was given to deep thought, and when he had persuaded Sylvia to marry him, it had seemed such a simple solution to both his problems. He would bring home a new wife, who might give him the heir he wanted and who meanwhile would be a good companion to his daughter.

"Perhaps I should have told her about you before hand," he mused. "Explained that I was bringing you home. It was all probably too sudden. However, she will become accustomed to the idea in time." Then he left for his study.

Yes, you should have prepared her for my coming, Sylvia thought. But she never said so.

What Martin had eventually said to placate his daughter, Sylvia was never told; from his future actions, she concluded that he had bribed the child with some expensive gift. It must have taken an even larger bribe, Sylvia decided, to persuade the child to give up her mother's room to her new stepmother.

After that time, Charlotte always behaved politely to her in Martin's presence. When they were alone, however, she made no secret of her hatred for her "new mama," knowing that Sylvia would say nothing to her father. At times, Sylvia suspected that Charlotte hoped she would speak of the girl's animosity; such a complaint could easily be twisted to make it seem that it was Sylvia who disliked her stepdaughter.

At first, Sylvia had wondered if the girl might have feared that the arrival of an infant brother would displace her in her father's affection. However, there never was a brother, and that had made no difference in Charlotte's behavior.

In the eighteen months since Martin's death, Charlotte had separated herself from Sylvia as much as possible. She went for long, solitary rides—despite frequent reminders that she should always be accompanied by a groom—or else spent her time in her room—even eating many of her meals there.

She had accepted the condolences of her friends quietly, merely biting her lips when one of them attempted to console her by saying, "But it is so good for you to have your dear mama to comfort you." Sylvia alone knew how the girl longed to say, as she had done when they first met, "She will never be my mama!"

Now, despite her sulkiness and her outward show of indignation at Sylvia for daring to put off her mourning, the older lady knew Charlotte was excited at the prospect of London Season. The mansion in Berkeley Square had now stood idle for more than two years—since the onset of Martin's long illness.

Now, looking around the house, Sylvia was happy to be back. The paper and the draperies had not suffered while the house had been closed. She would not have had the power to have any changes made, of course, since the house was no longer hers, but there was no need to do so. With the holland covers off the furniture, and the chandeliers and mirrors polished until they glistened, it would be the perfect spot from which Charlotte should enter the *ton*.

Her presentation should have taken place last year, but that would have been too soon after Martin's death. Seventeen was not too old for a young lady's come-out, but Sylvia knew it should not be put off any longer.

How fortunate it was for the success of her plans that the new earl was still living abroad, and they could use the house.

Even with the mansion at their disposal, there was much to be done. Charlotte's ball was to be one of the first large affairs of the Season. For that, and for the many affairs which would follow, both ladies must be properly gowned. To Sylvia, that meant Madame Celeste.

Had Charlotte been given a choice in the matter, she would doubtless have chosen some other couturiere but she forgot her sullenness when she saw the vast supply of materials Madame produced for their choice. No female could fail to be entranced by the lavish display. Every type of material was in evidence from the sheerest muslins to the heaviest brocaded satins, although the latter would scarcely be suitable for the present Season. Still, one could keep their beauty in mind for future occasions. There were even a number of delicately embroidered silk fabrics which clearly had come from France, despite the war.

"Why must everything be white?" Charlotte asked, turning over several of the figured materials.

"Because white is *de rigueur* for a young lady's debut," Madame explained, as if surprised that she should ask.

"For your first Season only," Sylvia said consolingly. "After that, you may wear colors."

It was a pity, she told herself, that Charlotte must be restricted to white. With her dark hair and blue eyes, she would look magnificent in brilliant colors. Still, her skin was clear and healthy, so she would not appear sallow in white as many dark-haired girls did.

"Actually, I prefer white," Charlotte announced. "But I should like to have at least one gown made up in lace."

Madame Celeste vigorously shook her head. "Never lace for a young girl," she said firmly. "Until you are married. *Then* you may wear it."

Sylvia braced herself for an explosion of anger, but Charlotte meekly accept the couturiere's statement as law, and went about selecting the materials for the various gowns. Seeing that the girl was willing to do as Madame Celeste decreed, Sylvia made no other suggestions.

Doubtless, Madame was well accustomed to handling willful young ladies. One obeyed her dicta or went to some lesser dressmaker for gowns. Since no one in the *ton* would risk being seen in other than the best, they meekly agreed to do as Madame said.

Although it was necessary for all the gowns to be white, it also proved to be the rule that there could be trimmings in colors: a tinted underdress, ribands, bunches of flowers, and embroideries of various kinds. Guided by Madame's good taste and with an income at her command to purchase whatever was thought necessary, Charlotte would be outfitted with the sort of wardrobe which would make the other young ladies cringe with envy.

Charlotte was so pleased with "her" choices that she made no objection when Sylvia began choosing the materials for her own gowns. Spoiled as she was, her good sense told her that her stepmother would have to dress properly to present her. Anything less would have shown to her disadvantage.

The days before her presentation ball seemed to fly by. The invitations had been sent and answered. Everyone of importance would attend the affair, with the exception of the members of "Carlton House set," to whom no invitations had been proffered. Martin had always sided with the King and Queen in the differences which arose in the royal family, and Sylvia thought it best to follow his lead. Even without the prince and his entourage, however, there would be a glittering assemblage for the ball.

Sylvia was putting the final touches to her personal preparations when Charlotte, who had been in an unusually benign mood all day, entered her room to show off her gown before going downstairs. The mood was broken as she halted in the doorway, staring at Sylvia, who was fastening her necklace.

"That was mama's necklace," the girl shouted. "You have no right to wear it. It should be mine."

Continuing to secure the clasp of the diamonds, Sylvia replied as calmly as she could. "You know better than that, Charlotte. True, they were your mother's jewels, but your father explained the matter to me—and to you—when he gave them to me. They are the traditional marriage gift to the Countess of Harmin."

"But my mama was the countess!"

"Yes, she *was*. As *I* now am, until your father's heir marries." She smiled at the girl encouragingly. "You do have all your mother's jewels at the bank vault. They will come to you when you marry."

"I would have them—now!" She then flounced from the room and Sylvia followed, sighing, as it seemed she did so often after an encounter with her stepdaughter.

She hoped that the excitement of being presented to the *ton* and having its members—especially its male members—make a fuss over her would serve to restore the girl's temper.

No doubt, Sylvia told herself, there would be some present who would disapprove of *her* appearance tonight. Some might be shocked to see that she had put aside her mourning, but the idea of swathing herself in black until she had followed Martin to the tomb—as she knew some ladies had done after their husband's death—made her shudder.

There was also the matter of her hair. An admirer had once told her that it was the color of ripened wheat on a sunny day. She remembered how she had laughed at the gallantry. But tonight her hair did look nice. She might be a widow, but she was only three-and-twenty, and had no intention of burying her hair beneath a cap and turban. Certainly not tonight. This might be her stepdaughter's come-out, but she wanted to look her best, as well.

The gown Sylvia had chosen for this evening was one of the same clear violet as her eyes. As she moved, the candlelight glinted upon the many silver threads with which it was embroidered, as well as upon the diamonds about her throat. At no more than three inches above five feet, Sylvia was aware that she could scarcely appear regal; yet her years as Countess of Harmin had given her a quiet dignity.

The young countess's eyes clouded for an instant as she looked at her stepdaughter moving about the floor. Charlotte had behaved properly when they had stood together, receiving the guests, then had willingly accepted several invitations to dance. Even in her First Season's white, there was something . . . something flamboyant about Charlotte's appearance. Not in her gown, certainly, and at this moment, not in her demeanor.

"What is it?" Sylvia asked herself, her gaze going from her stepdaughter to the other girls about the room. "Why is she different?"

Was it merely that none of them had hair so lushly black, eyes so startlingly blue, lips so naturally scarlet and full that they seemed to be begging to be kissed? Charlotte was a beauty, there was no doubt about that. And she was only too aware of her beauty—and its power.

"I was never half so certain of myself as she is, when I was seventeen—" But then, Sylvia had never been as indulged as Charlotte had been. Her own parents disapproved of showing their affection—in fact, Sylvia had often wondered if she had aroused the slightest affection in them—while Martin had never denied his daughter anything she desired.

"Except freedom from her stepmother, and he could never see how much she wanted that."

Sylvia forced these thoughts from her mind and smiled as Lady Sefton fluttered toward her. Lady Sefton was sweet—was by far the nicest of the "dragons" who guarded Almack's—but no one could deny that she fluttered.

"My dear Lady Harmin, how lovely you look tonight. But then, you always do."

She embraced Sylvia heartily, enveloping the younger lady in a wave of the delicate scent which was so much a part of her image. Not for her ladyship were the cloying perfumes that some ladies preferred.

"I may call you Sylvia, may I not, even though we have not met since you were a small child?" Sylvia smiled, knowing that she had seen the frequently forgetful lady at least half a dozen times in the days when she had come up to London as Martin's wife.

"Your vouchers for Almack's are assured, of course. Sally Jersey wanted to see to them for you, but I insisted on seeing to them myself. After all, your mama and I were bosom-bows when we were girls."

"How kind of you to say that," Sylvia said, knowing that her mother had been at least ten years older than Lady Sefton.

"We were, indeed, so close, while Sally was the merest acquaintance. Sally was such a *wild* girl, you know, one might almost say she was fast. And, just between the two of us," her voice dropped to a whisper, "she has not changed in the least, although she is now old enough to know better. Why, do you know they have been saying—"

"It is most kind of you to provide us with the vouchers," Sylvia broke in, embarassingly aware that there was a gentleman standing behind Lady Sefton who had overheard the *on-dit*, despite the lady's confidential tone.

# CHAPTER
## ❧ 2 ❧

Who was he? Sylvia wondered. The guest list for the ball had been chosen with care and she had at least a passing acquaintance with everyone on it. This was not someone she had once seen and had forgot. He was not a man one could easily forget.

There might have been gentlemen in the room who were more handsome, but after a glance at him, Sylvia did not see them. What there was about him that drew her attention, she could not have said. Certainly, it could not be any of the extravagance in dress that some gentlemen flaunted. Slightly above medium height, he was neatly but becomingly clad in midnight-blue coat and evening trousers. His cravat and shirt with its medium-high points were snowy and unadorned by any foppish displays of jewelry. Nor did he wear more than a single ring, a signet, she thought, and no quizzing glass hung about his neck.

There was something about his face that made her feel she would like to know this man better—yet she also sensed that he did not share her feeling. About his mouth and eyes were lines which told of frequent laughter, though now there was not even a shadow of a smile. His dark brown eyes were fixed upon her, but not with admiration.

Reluctantly becoming aware that her hostess's attention had strayed, Lady Sefton turned. Then she gasped and caught the gentleman by the hand, drawing him forward.

"My dear, I almost forgot—although how could anyone forget so handsome a gentleman—I knew you would not mind if I brought my guest this evening. Extra gentlemen are always welcome at a ball, are they not? Dear Sylvia, this is Mr. Bennett Griffith."

"Lady Harmin." His voice was as cold as the expression in his eyes as he stepped forward, barely touching the hand she extended to him.

His formal bow above her fingers was so brief as to approach insult. It was long enough, however, for Sylvia to feel an absurd desire to reach out her other hand to the back of his neck, where even the harsh Brutus cut could not prevent his dark hair from trying to curl. Instead, she clenched her fingers, forcing the hand to remain at her side. How could she imagine so gauche an action?

"Mr. Griffith." She struggled to match his cool tone, wondering why Lady Sefton imagined so rude a person would be welcome anywhere. Yet she *wanted* to welcome him, would happily have done so if his manner had not been so unpleasant.

"Dear Bennett's papa was a close friend of your late husband," Lady Sefton gushed, oblivious to the man's cool attitude. "So I know the two of you will be good friends. Bennett has just recently left the army, after having been wounded in battle—at Talaveras, was it not?"

The young man reluctantly nodded, as if he thought it impossible to break the flow of her conversation. Then her ladyship gave him a sharp glance. "Bennett— you are not wearing your sling," she said reproachfully.

"It is not truly necessary, and there is something rather ostentatious about wearing it in public. As if one wished to call undue attention to what is no more than a scratch." Sylvia wondered if the small scar beneath his left eye was another souvenir of that battle. She thought it enhanced his good looks.

"Your 'scratch,' as you call it, was enough to win your release from the service," Lady Sefton said sternly. "You must take good care of him, Sylvia, and see that he does not do too much. Oh, there is . . . I must . . ." Her words faded as she hurried off after another acquaintance.

Bennett and Sylvia stood in silence for several moments. When it seemed clear that he was not going to make an attempt at conversation, Sylvia said, "I presume, then, since your father was his friend, that you also knew my husband."

"Yes, I was acquainted with both the earl and countess."

"The *first* Lady Harmin, you mean?" she replied, stung. She had barely stopped herself from saying, "But *I* am the countess."

"You will forgive me, I am certain, if I cannot think of anyone taking her place." His tone showed quite clearly that he did not care whether or not she forgave him.

Sylvia could not control the anger which crept into her voice. "Then you and my stepdaughter should have a great deal in common."

"I am certain that we must have. I must be completely rude, Lady Harmin, and own that I came this evening only for the child's sake."

"I must say, at least, Mr. Griffith, that you are honest." The young countess felt her temper beginning to slip, a thing which seldom happened to her. After six years of Charlotte's antagonism, she had learned to keep it under strict control. But this gentleman had the ability to stir her emotions. "We have never met, yet it is clear that you dislike me. Perhaps you would be kind enough to tell me why."

His gaze went almost insolently from her head to her feet, then rose again to meet her own eyes. "I do not like cheats," he said bluntly.

"Cheats?"

"What would you call it?"

Her face turned scarlet. Was he alluding to the fact that she had not provided her husband with an heir to the earldom? If so, he was beyond outrageous. It had been a great sorrow to her, as well as to Martin, that they had never had a child—and not merely for the sake of the title. She had longed for children of her own, children who would love her as Charlotte had never done.

But how rude of a stranger to sit in judgment upon her? The hand which had lately been tempted to touch his hair now tingled with the urge to slap him soundly. Then she reminded herself firmly that she *was* Countess of Harmin and this man was a guest beneath her roof, although an uninvited one. She was determined not to make a scene. Yet, she was equally determined not to accept such censure from him.

She fixed a smile on her face. "If you have finished insulting me to your satisfaction," she said softly, "I should suggest that it might be wisest for you to take your leave as soon as possible, sir. I shall explain to Lady Sefton that you have suddenly recalled an urgent engagement elsewhere."

The scar beneath his eye showed more prominently as his face paled and his lips formed a thin, hard line. Although he must have expected a response, he clearly had not expected her to be a worthy adversary.

He bowed his acceptance of her dismissal and half-turned to take his leave. Then there was a shriek. "Bennett . . . Bennett, it *is* you!"

Ignoring the stares her behavior was causing, Charlotte came running across the floor toward him, both hands extended as if she intended to fling her arms about him. He caught her hands. Smiling, spreading her arms, he studied her from head to toe, but without any sign of the condemnation he had shown Sylvia.

"You have become a beauty," he said in warm tones. "I should never have known you. How have you been, brat?"

Charlotte stamped her foot. "How dare you call me that? I am not a brat. I never was."

"You were, my girl, definitely a brat. But quite a lovable one, I must say. And, although I can see that you have not outgrown that habit of stomping your foot when you are annoyed, you have become a lovely young lady while I was away. It will be a pleasure to dance with you."

"I do not know whether I wish to dance with you or not. You never wrote me—not once—during all the time you were away." She slipped her hand cosily beneath his arm as she spoke, giving him a smile which belied the criticism in her words.

As he looked from her stepdaughter to her, Sylvia saw the smile leave his face. With another half-bow, he said coldly, "Madam." Then the smile returned as he led the girl into the dance.

Sylvia grimaced as she looked after them. She hoped that after tonight they would not ever see that gentleman again.

Sylvia determinedly put the rude gentleman out of her mind as she mingled with her other guests. Her next obstacle would be Almack's, quite as important an occasion for the young lady as her Presentation Ball.

Compared to the Harmin mansion in Berkeley Square, or to any of the other fine houses in the city, the rooms in King Street were unpretentious indeed. A stranger, looking at their lack of adornment and uneven floors for the first time, might be excused for wondering what there was about this place which made it, after the royal dwellings, the most important spot in London.

In many minds, undoubtedly, it ranked above the palaces in importance. It was possible for one to survive in London without having entrée to the presence of royalty, but the young lady who was denied entrance to Almack's might as well retire to the country at once, for she would be received nowhere else.

From time to time, a gentleman might also be denied admittance, although in his case, the denial might be only temporary. The rules for the conduct of males were slightly more lenient, but if the reason was more serious than merely appearing in other than the proper dress, the results could be dire. One wag had written a verse which ended:

*But barred from there on Wednesday night,*
*By Jove, you can do nothing right.*

Just how this simple establishment had managed to attain such importance to members of the *ton*, no one could tell. Yet Almack's Patronesses included an Austrian princess, a Russian countess, several noble English ladies— and the extremely wealthy Mrs. Drummond-Burrell. Perhaps because she lacked a title, Mrs. Drummond-Burrell was the most autocratic of all. How many slight lapses by young ladies had been greeted by that Patroness's lifted eyebrows and her scathing *"Farouche!"*

But Sylvia had no reason to worry. As Lady Sefton had said, there had never been a doubt that the all-important vouchers would be provided for the Countess of Harmin and her stepdaughter.

The countess hoped that her stepdaughter would remember that she was not to waltz without permission, but knew any reminder on her part would doubtless drive the girl into doing exactly that, with no thought given to the results of her action.

Finally, Wednesday arrived. When they walked in Lady Jersey, as always, was very much in evidence. She hurried to meet them.

"You know that *I* wished to send you vouchers," she said, pausing in her speech long enough to have Charlotte presented to her, "but the little Sefton did so before I had the chance. Not that it matters, after all. You are here. And you look so lovely, child." As she looked from one to the other, it was difficult to tell whether the compliment was meant for Sylvia or Charlotte. "I *never* did so, even when I was your age."

Sylvia could believe that. Sally Jersey was sharp-faced and must have been so even as a child, although there were those who declared she had once been a beauty. Sylvia dimly recalled the lady's runaway marriage some years before her own, but could not feel that Lady Jersey had been more than average-looking at that time.

Despite her appearance, Lady Jersey could—and frequently did—boast of a number of amours, many of them with gentlemen in high places.

As was customary, the lady was overdressed in a brilliant yellow gown which, aside from its color, would have been more suitable for one of Charlotte's age. In her hair—which gossip said owed much of its color to the efforts of her coiffeur—she wore three large ostrich plumes that matched her gown.

Without being told, the Countess of Harmin was confident that *she* herself looked quite well turned out this evening. "Not at all widowish," she told herself. Her gown was of amber crepe, simply cut, and she wore no other jewels than the strand of large pearls Martin had given her.

"I am certain there must be a number of people here that you already know," Lady Jersey was continuing. "But many of the younger set will be new to you, my dear Sylvia, even though most of them are almost the same age as you. You must not play chaperon this evening; certainly, you do not look like one."

"I thank—"

"Pay no attention to Mrs. D–B if she frowns at you. You know she disapproves of everyone. And you need not concern yourself about your Charlotte; I shall see that she meets the proper young men."

She had caught Charlotte by the arm and was leading her away before the girl had time to agree with this plan. Not that Lady Jersey gave her an opportunity to protest. The lady's nickname of "Silence" had been truly earned if mockingly bestowed.

Her stepdaughter was quite the most beautiful girl in the room, Sylvia thought, glancing about at the bevy of hopeful young ladies. Tonight, the skirt of Charlotte's white gown was caught up in several places with bunches of flame-colored flowers, and some of the same flowers adorned her dark hair. The result was daring, almost on the edge of being too colorful for her first Season, but nonetheless, it quite suited Charlotte.

She, too, was wearing pearls, a smaller strand than her stepmother's. When Martin had given them to Sylvia, Charlotte had privately told her stepmother that she thought the large pearls much too vulgar for a lady; the implication was clear. Tonight, however, the girl was far too interested in her own success at Almack's to pay much attention to what her stepmother might be wearing.

Sylvia was approached almost at once by a gentleman with an invitation to the quadrille just forming. After the briefest of protests that she *should* take her place with the other chaperons, she allowed herself to be led to the floor. Whenever they met during the dance, he kept up a stream of heavy-handed compliments, which pleased her at first, but which soon became boring.

"Let me bring you a drink," he urged when the dance was finished.

"Thank you, I think not at present," Sylvia said, but he had darted away without waiting for her reply. He returned soon with a glass which he pressed awkwardly into her hand, nearly spilling it. Soon thereafter several acquaintances called to him asking him to settle their dispute.

The man guided Sylvia to the group of his friends. However, far from settling the matter, his rather inane chatter seemed to make things worse. Completely uninterested in what they were saying, she moved quietly out of hearing, sipping her orgeat, deciding she liked the faint almond flavor, after all.

"Insipid drink, is it not?" a voice said in her ear.

Sylvia turned about, expecting that she would see an old acquaintance, but the gentleman smiling down at her was certainly someone she had never met. Startled that a stranger should approach her without having been properly presented—here, of all places, where the rules of conduct were so rigidly controlled—she did not reply.

Quite as if she had spoken, he smiled again and went on, "But then, I suppose ladies appreciate such drinks as these." He tapped the edge of his lemonade glass with his elegant snuffbox. "However, I cannot understand how they could like the stale bread and butter or even staler cakes which are all one ever finds here."

"Then why do you come here, if you dislike it so?"

"I have often asked myself the same question. And it is only now that I found the answer."

# CHAPTER
## 🐾 3 🐾

*How impudent!* Sylvia started to frown at him, but felt her lips curving into a smile in response to his own. Doubtless, that was the effect he had on many ladies, she thought. He was quite tall—indeed, she had to tip her head far back to see his face. His hair was fairer than her own, and his features finely chiseled. Though her experience was limited concerning the proper dress for a gentleman, she thought he was impeccably attired. His evening coat and knee breeches were black, his white cravat adorned with a small jeweled pin. As he spoke, he pocketed the snuffbox, but fingered his quizzing glass.

"I have been making a nuisance of myself to all my friends—or so they tell me—begging them to present me to the loveliest lady in all of London. But alas, none of them appear to know you."

"I . . . I have been away from the City." Even as

she said the words, Sylvia wondered why she felt it necessary to offer any explanation. Even a close friend would hesitate to ask such personal questions.

"That accounts for what I should otherwise consider an unforgivable lapse on the part of my friends. Then, in the absence of those who might present me, may I present myself? Captain Hugo Lannon, who asks nothing better than to be at your service."

Have I been away too long? Sylvia wondered, to have forgot how people speak here in the City. Or is it just this man whose speech is so extravagant? No, her earlier partner had spoken extravagantly as well. But for some unexplainable reason, from this gentleman the words were more acceptable.

She knew she should tell him that he must apply to Lady Jersey or one of the other Patronesses to introduce him if he wished her acquaintance. Instead, she heard herself saying, "I am Lady Harmin."

"And is Lord Harmin with you tonight?" Was there just a shade of disappointment in his tone, or was that, too, a part of his pretense? Many gentlemen would not hesitate to begin a flirtation with a married woman.

She shook her head. "I am a widow."

"I think you must have been a child-bride." No sign of condolence in his tone. "But now, my lovely lady, will you dance with me?"

Should she stand up for a dance with a gentleman who had not been properly presented to her? And at Almack's, of all places? Of course, Sylvia told herself, she would do nothing of the kind. Then she became aware that the musicians had begun playing a waltz, and immediately looked anxiously about for Charlotte, afraid the girl might commit the error of waltzing without waiting for permission. It was a faux pas which some eager young ladies had committed from time to time—and a fatal one for their chances.

However, across the room Lady Jersey was presenting a young gentleman to Charlotte, apparently giving them her permission to waltz. The girl was looking properly grateful, even though her partner was a sandy-haired, rather awkward-appearing person. Sylvia sighed in relief.

At that moment, Lady Sefton entered the room, with Bennett Griffith at her side. Her ladyship waved to Sylvia and apparently prompted her companion's attention, for he looked in that direction, his expression as disdainful as before, despite his half-bow.

What right had he, a commoner, to sneer at her—and for so archaic a reason? For it seemed that he blamed her for the nonappearance of an heir to the earldom. Or had he some other reason for his dislike? Impulsively, Sylvia turned her back upon the pair and said, "I should be happy to dance with you, Captain Lannon."

His smile widened, showing beautifully formed teeth, and his arm went about her, drawing her among the dancers. "For a moment," he said, "I feared you were going to refuse to dance with me."

"For a moment, that was my intention."

"Then I must bless whatever it was which changed your mind."

He guided her skillfully among the other couples, their steps matching well despite the difference in their height. He was not in uniform, but remembering the manner in which he had introduced himself, Sylvia asked, "Captain Lannon? Were you in the army?"

"I have the honor to be a member of the Duke of Wellington's staff."

"Perhaps," she said, feeling daring, "that accounts for

your being such an excellent dancer. We have been told that His Grace would not have an officer on his staff who could not dance well."

"It is true that the Duke likes those about him to be able to be at home among the mighty. But there was little enough time for us to dance while we were on the Peninsula. We were kept busy trying to make the French dance to our tunes."

At once she was contrite. "I *am* sorry. I did not intend to make it sound as if you were frivolous. I am certain that you must have conducted yourself well, as did all our brave forces. We were not, however, as conversant with the progress of the war as if we had lived in London."

"If I did do well," he said smiling, "it was because there was far more danger in angering 'Old Douro' than in facing the French. But all that unpleasantness is in the past now that Bonaparte is safely caged. Let us speak of more pleasant things. How does it happen that London has not been favored by your presence until now? And why are we at last so fortunate?"

"I have been in mourning until recently. Now I am here to bring out my stepdaughter." She indicated Charlotte, who was striving rather unsuccessfully not to show her boredom at being partnered by a young man who seemed too busy counting his steps to give any attention to his partner. "It is a pity that she could not have had you as a partner for her first waltz. I am certain she would have found it much more enjoyable."

Laughing heartily as the music drew to a close, he turned and surveyed Charlotte through his quizzing glass, then smiled as if he approved of her. Sylvia wondered if he had surveyed her in the same manner before approaching her. "My dear lady, are you suggesting that I should ask her to stand up with me?"

Sylvia looked at him in surprise, then joined in his laughter. "I had not meant it in that way, sir, but only as a compliment to your skill. However, since you have spoken of it, I wish you will do so. Charlotte does dance well and I know you will enjoy partnering her."

"Not as much as I shall enjoy partnering you again. You will allow me another dance, will you not, Lady Harmin? Or several more?"

"One more only," the young countess said firmly. "Even in my position—perhaps I should say especially in my position—I cannot stand up for more than two dances in an evening with the same gentleman. As you must know."

"I know." He sighed so deeply that one could almost think he meant it. "But one can always hope for miracles."

He turned away and, on a sudden thought, she said, "Captain Lannon—"

The gentleman was at her side in a moment, asking, "Are you thinking better of sending me away?"

"No." He *was* impudent, but she had never known anyone who could make her laugh so often. "Only to remind you that you must be presented properly to my stepdaughter. You know the Patronesses would dislike it if you accosted her directly—although I do not think she would object." Any more than she herself had objected.

"As I said, I ask only to be of service to you. But I did not think the service would carry me so far from your side."

He spoke in tones of mock disappointment, but bowed deeply and strolled away to request Lady Jersey to present him to Charlotte, while Sylvia found another partner waiting to lead her out.

Some time later, Sylvia found herself standing beside Lady Sefton. "My dear," she said reproachfully, "I have been hoping to see you and dear Bennett sharing a dance. It would make me happy, and I know your dear husband would have wished you to be his friend. But you have been so busy all the evening."

Sylvia started to make some evasive reply; however, at that moment, Mr. Griffith came up with the lemonade he had fetched for her ladyship.

Seeing his expression tighten as he recognized her, Sylvia said, "You are kind to think of me, Lady Sefton. However, the truth of the matter is that Mr. Griffith has not asked me to dance."

Before the gentleman could protest that he had not yet had the opportunity to ask for a dance—an opportunity Sylvia was certain he did not wish—a voice behind her said, "And at any rate, Lady Harmin does not have this dance free to give. It is already promised."

Recognizing the voice, Sylvia turned to smile at the newly arrived gentleman. "Quite right," she said. "It is promised. Lady Sefton, I do not know if you are acquainted with Captain Lannon. He is a member of the Duke of Wellington's staff." As the captain bowed gallantly over the older lady's hand, complimenting her in a manner to make her smile upon him, Sylvia added, as if in afterthought, "And this is Mr. Griffith."

The two gentlemen eyed each other somewhat warily, and Sylvia received the impression that while Mr. Griffith certainly may not wish to dance with her himself, he was not pleased to have the other doing so. The thought made her smile again as she placed her hand upon her partner's arm and permitted him to lead her to the floor.

"I think I understand," he said, "that the gentleman

is not among your favorites." Then the pattern of the dance separated them.

"Nor I among his," she replied when they came together again.

"Then that is surely my good fortune." This made her laugh as they went their separate ways once more.

When the dance had ended and they stood together, he complained, "Surely that is not the only dance you will grant me. I wanted another waltz, so that I could hold you in my arms and tell you how beautiful you are."

Sylvia drew a sharp breath. Certainly the gentleman was being presumptuous beyond permission. Nothing she had said or done could have given him reason to think he could treat her in this manner. "The rule is two dances only," she reminded him, determined to remain polite, even in the face of such brashness.

"But why did you say you must be especially careful to obey it?"

"Can you not see? I have shocked almost everyone as it is by putting aside my mourning after no more than eighteen months. Even Charlotte—I should say, especially Charlotte—she sees my action as disrespect to her father. But she has accepted it because I must do so to bring her out. Once here, however, I am expected to sit among the chaperons, not to enjoy myself."

Captain Lannon looked at the solemn row of matrons and spinsters sitting along the walls, then looked down at her and shook his head.

"Rubbish, my dear, if you were ninety, you would not belong among such crows. And you need not try to convince me otherwise. Now, may I call upon you?"

Was it the fact that she *had* put off her mourning that had given these two gentlemen, both strangers to her, the right to treat her as they had been doing? Bennett Griffith made no secret of his dislike for her. Captain Lannon, on the other hand, had been behaving toward her with a freedom that showed a complete lack of respect.

"I do not think it would be wise for you to call." He looked crestfallen. She relented to say, "If I can persuade Charlotte that it is to her advantage to be seen there, we shall be driving in the Park tomorrow afternoon at the usual hour."

"Wonderful. I shall look forward to tomorrow. But could I persuade you to come alone?"

"Certainly not." How was she to convince him that she did not approve of such forward conduct? "I am in London to see to Charlotte's come-out. *She* is the one everyone is intended to see."

He sighed again in so melodramatic a fashion that she could not fail to be amused. "Very well," he said, "but I assure you that *I* shall not be there to see the chit. And I shall not pretend that I am."

Soon after that, he made his *adieux* and left the hall. Sylvia felt almost dizzy. Nothing of this kind had ever happened to her. Martin's suit had been ordered, unexciting.

A voice said in her ear, "I wonder what your husband would have said had he seen the way you have been behaving this evening. Or should I say *mis*behaving?"

She whirled about, although she had recognized the accusing voice.

"Or would he have been surprised?" Bennett Griffith went on. "Perhaps he was accustomed to such fast behavior."

"You may be thankful," she said fiercely, "that I wish to do nothing to spoil this evening for Charlotte. If it were not for that, I fear I should shock the Patronesses and the—" what had the captain called them? "—'the

crows' by slapping your face right here before everyone."

She started to walk away from him, but he caught her
wrist. At that moment, the music began again, another
waltz.

"No, you are not leaving so quickly," he said. "I wish
to talk to you."

"But I have no wish to talk to *you*."

Before she realized what he had in mind, however, he
swung her onto the dance floor, his arm gripped firmly
about her waist. "Smile," he ordered, "unless you wish
everyone to know we are quarreling."

"We are *not* quarreling, and I do not intend to dance
with you!" She tried to pull away, but he drew her
closer—much closer than was considered polite—and
spun her into the dance.

"I told you to smile," he ordered again. With a forced
smile upon his own face, he continued to guide her
smoothly about the floor. Observers would have thought
the words he was addressing to her were complimentary.
He might even have been forgiven—except by a few of
the highest sticklers—for the intimacy with which he
was holding her.

"What do you suppose Charlotte thinks of your
actions?" he ended his animadversion upon her behavior.
"Do you think she enjoys watching while her stepmother
blatantly searches for a new husband?"

"I am *not* searching for a new husband," Sylvia said
angrily. "And as for Charlotte, nothing would please her
more than to have me marry again and lose the allowance
Martin left me. Then everything that it was possible for
her father to leave would be her own and she need never
speak to me again."

"What?" He missed a step, causing her to stumble.

Pulling himself together, he guided her to the edge of the floor and took his arm from her waist, although he still held her arm. "Are you telling me that you did not manage to talk the earl into leaving you his property— or at least, its control?"

"I cannot see that the arrangements my husband might have made for my future are any of your affair, Mr. Griffith, since I have been given to understand that you are in no way related to the family. But since you seem determined to make them so, you may as well know the whole of them. Naturally, the title and most of the estates are entailed upon my husband's cousin—"

"Failing an heir."

"Failing an heir." She spoke between clenched teeth, no longer attempting to smile.

"The balance of his fortune," she continued, "will be Charlotte's. She will not be one of the great heiresses of the *ton*, of course, but she will have as much as she requires. I *am* in control of the estate for her until she comes of age or marries—which I can assure you she will do as quickly as she can. Then everything will be hers, except for the generous allowance my husband made for me. If I marry again, I shall forfeit that."

"I see." He gazed at her thoughtfully. "Then it will be greatly to your advantage, will it not, to find a wealthy husband?"

"I believe you have said quite enough, Mr. Griffith. If you will have the goodness to take your leave of me, we may escape without a scene, after all."

For a moment, it seemed he would say something more, something equally as insulting as his earlier comments, she was certain. Then he made a half-bow. Sylvia attempted to retain the feeling of anger he had aroused in her, but was forced to own that if it had not been for his censorious speeches, she doubtless would have enjoyed the dance. Even more, she suspected, than the dance she had shared with the captain.

This was a ridiculous idea, she told herself. She knew she could not like anything that man might do. Later, as she let herself into the house in Berkeley Square, she decided the entire evening had been most unsettling. Charlotte's night, however, had been a success. She danced every dance. Had that not been the purpose of the evening?

Sylvia decided to concentrate on more pleasant thoughts, like the drive in the Park she would be taking the next afternoon. Not that she hoped to meet the captain, she told herself. He was far too brash and unmannerly. But if he should be there . . .

# CHAPTER
## ❧ 4 ❧

He was there, accompanied by two friends, whom he reluctantly introduced as Lieutenant Forrest and Sir Wallace Pember.

"Ran into the pair of them at the club," he confided, "and could not get away from them, no matter how hard I tried to do so."

"Certainly not," Sir Wallace told him, "when we knew you were going to meet a beautiful lady."

"I did not tell you anything of the kind," Captain Lannon protested.

"No, I own that you did not," the lieutenant agreed with a grin. "You were quite careful to say nothing to us of your plans for this afternoon. That is so unusual for you that we knew you had something like this in mind."

Sylvia was amused by their raillery, but soon Sir

Wallace and the lieutenant were hailed by others they knew and rode off, chaffing their friend as they went. On the other side of the carriage, Charlotte was happily holding court among a group of four young gentlemen, all vying for her undivided attention. At Sylvia's request, the girl, aware that it would be impolite to the gentlemen if she did not do so, named them, but so rapidly that Sylvia could hardly understand the names.

"Certainly, we shall be at home tomorrow," she heard Charlotte say.

She remembered a dressmaker's appointment that she would now have to cancel since all the young men had been quick to accept the invitation. Sylvia turned to the captain, asking, "Would you like to call, sir, and perhaps bring your friends as well?"

"You know I should prefer to come when they do not," he said boldly.

She shook her head and frowned, and he went on quickly, "But of course, I shall come then—if that is the only time you will allow me."

Beyond him, at that moment, she saw another rider pass. Recognizing her—or more probably, she thought, he had seen Charlotte—Bennett Griffith drew his steed to a halt and half-bowed at her above its back. Sylvia was about to pretend that she had not seen him, then impulsively gave him a smile and a nod of recognition. He appeared somewhat surprised at her reaction, but Sylvia thought he was pleased.

He must have thought it showed that she did not bear a grudge for his criticism of her actions. How little the gentleman knew of her true feeling toward him.

Riding to her side of the carriage, Bennett said, "I heard Charlotte say you would be at home on the morrow. May I call, as well?"

Sylvia paused only a moment. "Certainly," she told him. "Martin's friends will always be welcome."

So now he was willing to be friends, was he, despite all the things he had said to her? Or was it merely that he was attempting to keep an eye on her for her stepdaughter's sake? Well, whatever he planned, *she* had a plan in mind which would not please the gentleman in the least—even though it would please her a great deal.

Busy with her schemes to bring Bennett Griffith to his knees—certain that shaming him would make her forget him—Sylvia scarcely noticed some of the people whom they met during the remainder of the drive, although she managed to reply so pleasantly to all greetings that no one was aware of her preoccupation.

As they left the Park, however, she was abruptly brought out of her thoughts by the sight of a roughly clad red-faced man on the walk, who was holding a cowering boy by one arm and whom he was belaboring with a large stick. "Halt the carriage at once, Edmonds, and stop that man from abusing the child."

"Oh no, milady, I could not do that. Doubtless, the boy is bound to him, and he'd not take kindly to anyone who tried to interfere."

"Well, if you will not—" Before the servant could say more, Sylvia had dismounted and approached the pair. As the man raised his stick to administer another blow, she poked him sharply in the ribs with her parasol. "Stop that at once," she ordered.

Whirling to face her, the man said belligerently, "What's it to you? He pinched my wallet—and that's a hangin' offense. He's lucky if I let him off with no more than a thrashin'."

"I never!" the boy cried. "I never touched it. You can see—He still has it."

"Well, he was a–goin' to take it, only I caught him before he could get his hands on it."

The boy continued to protest his innocence, but the man only shouted louder.

"If he has not stolen anything, you have no right to beat him," Sylvia commented.

"This ain't none of your affair, and I ain't lettin' no gentry-mort give me orders." He turned angrily toward her. The boy, taking advantage of the distraction, slipped from his hands and disappeared among the crowd which had gathered, eager for the sight of any kind of trouble. "Now, look what you done," the self-styled victim raged, his wrath turned against Sylvia for her interference. "You've let a thief get away."

"There was no proof that he was a thief."

Her calm statement infuriated him further and he started toward her, so that she was forced back against the side of the carriage. Edmonds might not have been willing to take the part of a ragged urchin, but his mistress was a different matter. He leaped to the ground, brandishing his whip. The other man then took to his heels as quickly as the boy had done.

Bennett Griffith had seen Lady Harmin leave her carriage to accost the man, and quickly turned his horse in that direction, trying to force a path through the interested onlookers. She was a little idiot, he told himself, attacking a brute like that. Someone should help her before the fellow turned upon her.

Before he could make his way through the crowd, however, the lady returned to her carriage and drove away as if nothing had occurred. Bennett looked after her, shaking his head. Who would have thought she would be so considerate of a ragamuffin?

*   *   *

Bennett Griffith's kind thoughts about the lady were
not shared by Charlotte. "I should have thought, Sylvia,"
Charlotte said in a censorious tone, "that even you would
not wish to bring such attention to yourself. Brawling in
a public place."

"I was scarcely brawling," her stepmother said. "And
I do not like to see anyone being abused. Especially one
who does not deserve such treatment."

"You could not know that he did not deserve it. He
might have been a *thief*—or worse!"

Sylvia sighed. "I doubt if one so young could be very
bad. But what does it matter? It is done, and we now
have more important things to concern us. The number
of callers we might expect tomorrow, for one thing."

As she had hoped, the thought of so many atten-
tive young gentlemen was enough to divert Charlotte's
thoughts from the earlier scene, and the two could now
plan for the morrow.

Wisely, Sylvia sent messages to several friends she
had met again last evening, telling them that the Countess of Harmin and Lady Charlotte would be at home on
the morrow and asking the ladies and their daughters to
call if they had not made previous plans. She doubted
Charlotte had thought to invite any of the young ladies
she had met, for they had spoken to no one during their
ride, but it would not be the thing for the countess and
her stepdaughter to be entertaining only gentlemen callers. Such behavior would be considered too bold.

"A very wise step, my dear," Lady Sefton wrote in
reply. "I must make other calls, but I shall stop, if only
for five minutes."

Sylvia sighed in relief when she received the message.
Despite the suddenness of the invitations, Lady Sefton's

presence would do much to put the stamp of propriety
upon the occasion.

The next day, when Bennett Griffith surrendered his
hat to Porton, the countess's butler, and was announced,
he entered the drawing room just as her ladyship was
leaving. "Oh, Bennett," Lady Sefton exclaimed, tapping
his arm, "I am happy to notice that you are renewing
your friendships here."

"You must remember that my previous friendship was
only with Lady Charlotte, Lady Sefton," he said. "I had
never met the present countess until you introduced us
at Charlotte's ball."

"That is so, I forgot. But no matter. You find her
charming, I am certain. And she has been away from
London for so long that she is in need of good friends,
she will be happy to see you. But now, I must rush—
I am promised at the Russian Embassy—It is certain to
be a stuffy affair, but one must do all that is required. I
shall see you again." She was gone before Bennett could
say more.

Sylvia noticed the gentleman's ill-concealed look of
surprise as he viewed the respectable dowagers and
young ladies who were mingled with the crowd of
beaux. So he still was uncertain about her, was he?
Well, he would learn. She had planned a painful lesson
for him.

He would apologize for the cruel things he had said
and thought about her. She was not quite certain how
she would bring this about, but she determined that his
penitence would be truly abject. *Then* she would inform
him that he was no longer welcome in her home. When
she had put him out of her house, she would then put
him out of her thoughts, as well.

She could not know that the gentleman had witnessed

her encounter outside the Park yesterday and was looking forward to today's meeting with pleasure. Whatever her object had been in snaring the earl, it would appear that the lady possessed some good qualities, he admitted. Her consideration for the boy and her pluck in confronting the bully were admirable.

Mr. Griffith made his manners to both the dowagers and the young ladies present, dismissing the crowd of young bucks about Charlotte with no more than a grin and a shrug. It would have been exceptional if so beautiful a young lady did not have a throng of admirers.

Oddly enough, it seemed to Sylvia, Mr. Griffith appeared to have overlooked completely the most handsome man in the room, the one man who was paying no attention to Charlotte. It was clear that Captain Lannon, however, was more observant.

"Do not tell me that I have a rival," he whispered.

Sylvia smiled at him, amused by his audacity. "A rival, sir?"

"For your affections."

She raised her brows. "You are much too forward, I fear, Captain, and if I were wise, I should forbid you to come here again."

"You could not be so cruel," he protested, his smile belying his hurt tone.

"I fear I am not as wise as I should be," she replied, answering his smile as well. The man was a rogue, but she was forced to own, an amusing one. And it was quite pleasant to hear his compliments, although she knew he did not mean them.

The captain drew a deep sigh of relief, although she was certain he was prevaricating. "I was worried for a time. Now tell me, what may I do in order to oust the gentleman?"

"If you are referring to Mr. Griffith, sir, you need have no fear. His father was my husband's friend, and he has known Charlotte since she was a child. He comes here merely for her sake. I met him for the first time at her Presentation Ball."

Why was she telling him all this? she wondered. He was as much a stranger as Mr. Griffith—more so, in fact, since he could not claim even a slight acquaintance with the family.

Several of the ladies rose to take their leave and to invite Sylvia and Charlotte to affairs of their own. They gave the captain sharp glances, but only two of them included him in the invitations, the others making a point of ignoring him.

He smiled and shook his head. "Always my fate, it seems. Too many ladies see a uniform—they know I possess one, even if I am not wearing it at the moment— as a threat to their daughters' virtue. As if one would bother with any of the chits. Lady Arlington, however, has no fear, as her daughter is already safely promised— to a nonentity, of course, but it means that she sees me as no threat. May I escort you to her rout?"

"I . . . I do not think it wise for me to accept, or even to consider such an invitation. I attend these affairs only on my stepdaughter's behalf. But perhaps we shall see you there."

"You may be assured of that." He bowed over her hand, brushed it with his lips, and took his leave. Sylvia turned back to her other guests and found Mr. Griffith was standing near her.

"Hardly the sort I should have chosen for you," he commented. Despite his careless appearance, he had known quite well that Captain Lannon was not here to pay court to Charlotte, but to her stepmother, and all his earlier pleasant thoughts about the lady had vanished when he saw that gentleman's attentions were apparently not repulsive to her.

To himself, he owned that he could not have blamed the captain for his interest in Lady Harmin, for the lady was lovely indeed. She must have been a mere child, he thought, at the time of her marriage. But even a child could be cruelly greedy. As she must have been, to have tricked the earl. Harmin had been no dolt, but doubtless was at the age where he could be fascinated by an attractive young chit.

Unaware of his thoughts, but still certain of his disapproval, Sylvia gave him her brightest smile. "Do you think so?"

"Or perhaps I am in error. You may find a soldier most fascinating."

"I suppose I do, in common with many ladies. But only *some* soldiers."

He ignored the barb. "But given what you have told me about losing your allowance from your late husband should you marry again, I should think you would be looking for someone with more substance."

How long, she wondered, could she keep her smile in place? "It is so kind of you to give me the support of your advice."

He half-bowed. "How could I do less for Harmin's widow—and for Charlotte's stepmother?"

"However, if I should find myself in need of advice, you may be certain I shall ask you for it." Her earlier plan to bring him to her feet was almost forgot for the moment. How dare he criticize her behavior? "I think, sir, it would be advisable for you to take your leave at once. You have already overstayed your welcome."

He laughed harshly. "I understand you completely,

my girl. Anyone who can see through your wiles would surely be unwelcome in your home. It is a pity that you have the ruling of Charlotte."

Her words followed him as he turned to take his leave, "Perhaps you should offer for her. Then she would be free of me."

Turning back, he said, "I should think, considering your opinion of me, that I would be the last person whom you would wish her to choose for her husband."

"On the contrary, I think the two of you would be perfectly matched! Now, I must not neglect my other guests; Porton will see you out."

The butler was at his side at that moment, the gentleman's hat in hand. Almost before he realized it, Bennett Griffith found himself on the sidewalk, fuming. Order him away, would she?

Then he began to grin. He was fully aware of the attraction he held for a number of young ladies, and felt certain he could beat this one at her own game. If he courted her with determination, he could win her. Then when he had shown her to the *ton* as the husband-hunting witch he knew her to be, he could laugh at her as she was doubtless laughing at him this moment.

That evening, Porton took an enormous bouquet from a footman and bore it into the small drawing room. Sylvia looked up from the magazine she had been perusing to comment, "It would seem that Lady Charlotte has another ardent admirer."

"No, milady, not on this occasion. The message is addressed to you."

From Captain Lannon, she supposed; it was like him to act so extravagantly. To her surprise, however, the message read, "My dear Lady Harmin, I am aware that I was unforgivably rude to you today. Please accept these flowers with my humblest apologies. Bennett Griffith."

Sylvia crumpled the notepaper in her hand, tempted to toss it into the fireplace. "Throw the flowers into the street," she ordered. Then, as Porton turned to obey, she said quickly, "Wait. The flowers are beautiful, and it is not their fault that their sender is . . . Have one of the maids arrange them in a vase. Or in several, if it is necessary."

Ladies—even the best of them, as he considered her ladyship to be—were unpredictable, the butler thought, turning to carry the flowers from the room, then stepping back to allow Charlotte to enter.

"What beautiful flowers!" she exclaimed, reaching for them. "Was there a card enclosed?"

"No . . . that is, yes, Lady Charlotte. There was a message. But the flowers are for her ladyship—for Lady Harmin."

Charlotte drew back her hand quickly. "Ostentatious, are they not?" There was a sneer in her voice.

"I am in complete agreement with you," Sylvia told her with a smile, wondering if Charlotte's feeling would be the same if she knew from whom the flowers had come. "However, we shall keep them."

Followed by the butler, Sylvia left the room, unaware that she had dropped the crumpled note. Charlotte spied it at once. Wondering who could have sent so large a bouquet—larger than anything *she* had even received—to her stepmother, she snatched up the paper.

Bennett! He was *her* friend, not Sylvia's! Why should he send flowers to her stepmother? Perhaps he had merely made a mistake, and had intended the flowers for her. Was there a chance that he had written "Lady Harmin" instead of "Lady Charlotte"?

A quick reading of the message dispelled that idea, but increased her curiosity. What could he have said to Sylvia to deserve an apology? "Whatever it is, I hope he repeats it often," she muttered, folding the paper and concealing it in her handkerchief. She would have to learn what he had said; perhaps it was something she could use against her stepmother one day.

# CHAPTER
## ❧ 5 ❧

Sylvia put the message and its sender from her mind as she prepared for Lady Arlington's rout. Tonight, she wore a gown of ice-blue net over a slip of satin in a slightly darker shade. A double row of pale pink rosebuds extended from her waist to her hemline, then continued around the scalloped hem of the net. A tiara of the same buds was set before the coils of her golden hair.

She ignored the frowns of some of the dowagers, who appeared to expect that she would take her place among them. As the mother—the stepmother, actually—of one of the young ladies, she was expected to be no more than a part of the background. Yet she saw no reason why she should do so. Not even the Patronesses—some of them, at least—at Almack's had expected that of her.

Of course, she would do nothing that would reflect badly upon Charlotte—Mr. Griffith's apparent expectations to the contrary—but after all, she had scarcely made her own come-out before she was married; this was her first true opportunity to enjoy herself.

As promised, Captain Lannon was present at the rout. He came to her side the moment she and Charlotte entered the room, closely followed by Lieutenant Forrest and Sir Wallace Pember. They were soon joined by a number of other gentlemen, each eager to be introduced to her.

Although Sylvia was flattered by so much attention, she encouraged most of the gentlemen to beg Lady Arlington to introduce them to Charlotte. The girl would not have welcomed them, she knew, if they were presented by her stepmother.

Reluctantly they left her, a few at a time, to meet Charlotte, to learn what balls she might plan to attend during the coming weeks, and to beg her to save them dances at those times. They asked her to promise to ride with them in the Park some day soon, and some of the bolder ones hinted that she might allow them to sit with her at supper.

Surrounded by her own crowd of admirers, Charlotte had scarcely appeared to notice when these gentlemen left her and drifted back in her stepmother's direction. But in fact, she was acutely aware of every moment's attention Sylvia was receiving. She saw Bennett come into the room, saw that he glanced toward the group about her stepmother, but smiled a welcome when he came toward her instead of joining Sylvia's admirers. Again she wondered what he could have done to anger her stepmother.

Sylvia too was also aware of Mr. Griffith's arrival, but she turned away when he looked toward her, pretending an intense interest in the conversation eddying about her. Hugo Lannon, in turn, had noticed the other gentleman, and the lady's reaction to his arrival as well. He continued his inconsequential chatter, but when Sylvia accepted his arm to the supper room, he said in a low tone, "Can it be that I no longer have a rival?"

"I beg your pardon?" She knew precisely what he meant, but pretended otherwise.

"Mr. Griffith no longer appears to be in your good books."

"I have told you before that his father was a friend of my late husband, and that he and my stepdaughter are old friends."

"And no friend of hers can be a friend of yours?" There was satisfaction in his tone.

Sylvia laughed, eager to turn the question aside. What she might think of Bennett Griffith was really not this gentleman's concern. "Have I not encouraged you to become her friend as well as mine?"

"I own that you have done so, and I danced with her because that was what you wished. But I still prefer to choose my own . . . friends. And you must know by this time that it is not friendship I wish from you, but something more."

"Really, sir, you must know that there are times when you go far beyond the line." It was fortunate that the detestable Mr. Griffith had not been near enough to overhear such a remark. It would have given him some excuse for his accusations of improper conduct on her part.

Captain Lannon bowed his head. "I abase myself and beg you to forgive me." But he smiled as he spoke, and Sylvia did not think his apology a whit more serious than his earlier remarks. If he were truly as boyish as he appeared at times, she would label him a scamp. But certainly he was not as young as that.

Still, she laughed. "Very well, I shall forgive you—this time. But on the condition that we have no more such talk."

"As you wish, my lady, but you must understand that this leaves me with very little to say."

"Good," she said heartlessly, and turned to speak to some friends who had joined them. At least, Bennett Griffith had made no attempt to come near her this evening or to show his disapproval. It gave her a pleasurable feeling to know she had put him in his place.

When his bouquet arrived the next morning—this one as large as the first—she wondered if it were merely coincidence that the roses were the precise shade of pink as the rosebuds on her gown last evening. "Surely he did not pay that much attention to me. Or did he do so?" she murmured, crumpling the message accompanying the flowers without troubling to read it. Doubtless, it was in the same vein as yesterday's, an attempt to overcome her dislike, but, she was certain, with no true meaning to it.

Lady Claridge's Venetian breakfast was one of the first of the Season. It was to be an *al fresco* affair, and both Sylvia and Charlotte were looking forward to it. The weather, however, refused to cooperate with her ladyship's plans. Suddenly, rain soaked the lawns, so that the servants had to hurry to save the food which had been spread lavishly about. The guests were forced to take refuge indoors, deprived of an opportunity to admire the decorative grounds, as the lady had intended.

Baron Claridge took advantage of this arrangement to collect a number of the gentlemen in the billiard room, where he handed about lavish glasses of potently doctored punch and regaled them with stories most of them had heard repeatedly during the past several Seasons. Her ladyship's messages—conveyed at intervals by the butler and becoming increasingly insistent—that the guests were expected in the drawing room were blithely ignored. The baron seldom had a captive audience. From time to time, however, some of them, convinced that even the punch did not make the stories more bearable, managed to slip away and make their way to join the ladies.

Bennett was one of these. He had not had the misfortune to be exposed to most of Lord Claridge's tales, as had some of his friends, but they differed little from army gossip, so he concluded he was missing nothing if he heard no more.

He stepped into the hallway, then halted to permit a procession of young maids bearing tea and various sweetmeats into the roomful of ladies. The last of the servants, seeming to struggle under the weight of her burden, entered the room just as Charlotte rose to her feet.

The collision was inevitable. The tray, with its load of chocolate-covered cakes, was flung against Charlotte's skirt, depositing its load from waist to hem before falling to the carpet. The young maid shrank back, her hands over her mouth, at the sight of the furious guest who now turned upon her, shrieking, "You clumsy dolt! Why did you not look where you were going?"

"I . . . I . . . Sorry, milady, I—" The girl clearly was too frightened to speak.

Sylvia went to her side, but Lady Claridge was already there. "A thousand pardons, Lady Charlotte. The girl will be dismissed at once."

"No, you must not, Lady Claridge," Sylvia exclaimed. "She was not to blame for what happened; there was no way she could have known that Charlotte was going to move at that moment."

"It is a servant's place to watch such things," Lady Claridge retorted, resentful of what she considered a lecture about the proper treatment of servants.

"And look what she did to my gown," Charlotte added. "I shall never be able to wear it again."

Since she had never worn the same gown a second time since they came to London, her stepmother said, "It is only a gown; you have any number of others. It is not right that a poor girl should lose her employment because of it."

"Nonetheless, she shall go at once," Lady Claridge said. "And without a character."

"In that case, Lady Claridge, since Charlotte will wish to change her gown, I am certain that you will excuse us if we leave at once."

Belatedly recalling her guest's superior position, Lady Claridge said lamely, "I regret that such a thing happened, Lady Harmin, but you can understand how difficult it is to get competent help."

"Indeed I do, so you will not mind if we take the girl with us, will you?"

Charlotte was so shocked she could not say anything for the moment. Sylvia hurried her out of the house, calling to the maid to accompany them. "What is your name, child?" she asked.

"Betsy, milady, but I—"

"Then, Betsy, you may come with us. We know you did not mean any harm, and should not suffer because of it. Edmonds, it is no longer raining so you may help the girl up beside you."

As the coachman obeyed with an air that said anything might be expected of Quality, Sylvia entered the
carriage, bracing herself for Charlotte's tirade. "It was
humiliating to me for you to take that creature . . . after
what she had done," Charlotte said furiously.

"All the girl did was to follow the other maids into
the room. She should not have to lose her employment
because of it."

"Well, I hope you do not think I shall allow her to
serve in my home."

"Our home—at least for the present. And you need
not see her, so you may as well forget the incident."

Charlotte lapsed into sulky silence until they reached
their town house, then went directly to her room. Sylvia
entered the small room she had set aside for a study and
summoned the butler. He came in, looking somewhat
startled at the maid, who was sitting on the edge of her
chair as if she might bolt at the first opportunity.

"I regret to say that I have created something of a
problem, Porton," Sylvia began. "I fully realize that it is
the province of you or Mrs. Hopgood, the housekeeper,
to employ new servants, and I should not wish to cause
any dissension in the household—But I wish you will
try to find a place in the house for Betsy."

"A place, milady? Here? I do not think we are in need
of more maidservants."

"I did not think you would be, for the service has been
excellent. But the poor girl has been dismissed from
her last place merely because she happened to be in
Lady Charlotte's way, with the result that Lady Claridge
blamed the girl for the ruin of Charlotte's gown."

Porton nodded; he had experience with the younger
lady's spells of temper and could sympathize with anyone who fell afoul of her. Still . . .

"If your ladyship would permit a suggestion. Perhaps there is another way to help her. My brother is butler for the Hendrickson family, and I happen to know that they are in need of a schoolroom maid. But if the young person cannot be recommended—"

"I can understand that requisite, but my recommendation would be sufficient, would it not?"

"Certainly, milady. And if you wish, I shall send a message to my brother at once, suggesting . . . uh . . . Betsy for the position."

"That will serve nicely, Porton." Sylvia sighed with relief. The poor girl would not be without employment. "Go with Porton," she ordered Betsy. "He will see you to your new position."

As he left the Claridge mansion, Bennett Griffith found himself in a state of complete confusion. Just when he was certain he understood Lady Harmin's motives for her marriage to his father's friend, the lady did something that revealed her in a totally different light. Would an entirely selfish person, such as he had been envisioning her, come to the aid of a servant, as she had done today at the breakfast?

In fact, it had been Charlotte who had incurred his displeasure on that same occasion. He had been a witness to the accident and knew the maid had not been to blame. But he knew it was customary for Quality to dismiss summarily anyone who caused a moment's unpleasantness for a guest. Sylvia's action in coming to the servant's defense was an unusual act for one of her position; her taking the maid away with her, doubtless with the intention of employing her, was even more so. Could he have been mistaken about her all this time?

He determined he would soon learn the truth about the lady. When they met at Madame Smitson's ball that evening, he bowed deeply to Sylvia, who awarded him a brief nod, although she still refused to smile or to thank him for his flowers. He need not think her forgiveness was that easily won.

The nod, however, was enough to cause Bennett to smile to himself. She might pretend haughtiness, he thought, but he had no doubt he would soon bring her around. But he asked himself if his motive for bringing her around was the same as it had been. After what he had today seen of her character, did he truly wish to discredit her with the *ton*?

This was the second time, he reminded himself, that he had seen her assist someone who was being mistreated. "No," he muttered to himself, "I do not think I wish to cause the lady to lose her standing with her friends." And he smiled again.

The smile broadened the next evening when he saw that the flowers she was wearing had certainly come from the bouquet he had sent that morning. But he walked away and asked Charlotte to dance with him.

Bennett was an excellent dancer, Charlotte mused, even for a gentleman who must have reached his thirtieth year. He was so easy to talk to as well, but she tried vainly to learn what he had said to anger Sylvia so deeply. "I think you might tell me," she coaxed. "After all, we are in complete agreement about the creature."

"That is no way to speak of your mother," he chided, thinking that *someone* had neglected to teach the girl proper manners. Her unnecessary anger at Lady Claridge's servant, and now her scathing reference to Sylvia, showed a lack of consideration for others which must be deplored.

"She is *not* my mother!" Charlotte said, quite as furiously as she had declared herself to Sylvia when Lord Harmin had first brought her stepmother home. If Bennett was going to speak to her in such a way . . . She attempted to wrench herself away, but he held her tightly.

"Very well, your father's wife," he amended.

"Yes—And I know you do not approve of that any more than I do."

"How I may feel about Lady Harmin, my girl, is no affair of yours." Truthfully, he was no longer certain exactly how he did feel about the lady, but, as he told Charlotte, it was not her affair. "And you will say no more about it."

"But Bennett—"

"You heard me." He twirled her about as the music ended, then released her. "I will not have you interfering with my plans. And do not sulk and stamp your foot, or you will frighten away the young man who is just about to ask you for the next dance."

Charlotte obeyed, although she wished to continue the conversation. There was time enough, she told herself, for her to learn what he had in mind. She flashed her brightest smile at the young gentleman approaching and permitted him to lead her out for the next country dance.

Sylvia had been aware that Charlotte and Mr. Griffith had had a disagreement, but was pleased that the girl had not gone into a fit of sulking about it. At least, no one could find fault in her stepdaughter's manners when a gentleman was present.

What could the pair of them have been discussing, Sylvia wondered briefly. Charlotte usually found Bennett in sympathy with whatever she might say, especially if she was complaining about her stepmother.

Seeing that same gentleman look in her direction, she nodded and smiled. The continued arrival of his bouquets made it appear that he did indeed regret his earlier unpleasant speeches, and she remembered her resolve to bring him to her feet so that she could dismiss him. But it no longer seemed worth the effort; she would treat him as she would any other gentleman she met during the Season—as long as he did not repeat his unkind remarks.

After all, she reminded herself, he was one of the best dancers she had met since coming to London. Even better than Captain Lannon.

That handsome gentleman was not present at every event they had attended, since there were always a number of balls and routs taking place at any one time, and it was impossible for him to guess at which ones they would appear. However, when they did meet, he was never far from her side for the balance of the evening, and Sylvia knew she could look forward to seeing him whenever she and her stepdaughter drove in the Park. Now and then, he was accompanied by various friends—possibly other soldiers, Sylvia thought—but more often, he appeared alone to ride beside their carriage.

Charlotte had attempted on several occasions to win his attention away from her stepmother, but when she found that impossible, she had begun snubbing him, feeling that anyone who preferred Sylvia's company to her own was beneath her notice.

The captain was well aware of her reaction, but was only amused by it. Such young ladies held no interest for him. He had made no secret that it was the countess who was the object of his attentions, and he was pleased to see that she did not appear to take exception to his pursuit. He was so pleased, in fact, that he determined to put his fortune to the test at the ball given by Lady Melbourne.

# CHAPTER
## ❧ 6 ❧

Unaware of what lay before her, Sylvia had nonetheless dressed with extreme care for this event, choosing a gown of blue brocade, its skirt trimmed with rouleaux of a darker material surmounted by a double row of white flowers. Not even to herself would she own that there might be a deeper reason for her interest in her appearance. She knew that Mr. Griffith would be present this evening. Certainly he would seek her out for a dance or two, as he had been doing at these past affairs.

She did not doubt that he enjoyed these dances as much as she, but she would not give him the pleasure of learning she thought him quite the best dancer she knew. And, although she would not yet own it, even to herself, there was an excitement in being

held in his arms as they whirled about the floor. It
was a feeling she did not experience with any other partner, not even with so skillful a dancer as the
captain.

It amused her to note the number of occasions during
the past evenings on which Mr. Griffith had swept her
away just as Captain Lannon could be seen approaching to beg for her company. Certainly, the gentleman
could not be jealous of her attentions to the captain, but
was it possible that he was beginning to become . . .
interested?

During the last dance, a careless partner had trod upon
the hem of her new gown just as she was rising to join
him on the floor. She did not allow the accident to
deprive him of her company. But after he had returned
her to her seat, she had retired to the cloakroom to
make certain he had not torn the hem or ripped any
of the rouleaux apart from her skirt. To her relief, she
found that his clumsiness had not even left a mark
upon the brocade, and she descended once more to the
ballroom.

She stopped for a moment at the foot of the stairs to
inhale the scent from a bank of fresh flowers separating
the room from the hallway, then realized the blossoms
hid her from a pair of gentlemen seated some distance
from the dancers. Recognizing from their voices Sir
Wallace and Lieutenant Forrest, neither of whom she
had seen for several days, she was on the verge of
stepping forward and greeting them, when she realized
that they were discussing her in low tones.

" . . . the pretty widow Harmin," the lieutenant was
saying.

"The pretty, *rich* widow Harmin, you mean," Sir

Wallace amended. "Certainly, Lannon fell into a fortune when he met her."

"No, you must own that Lannon has always made his own fortune when it comes to the females. Do not doubt he could have the pick of the lot, even if some of the mothers warn their daughters against soldiers. As we have reason to know. But Hugo always swore that when he got buckled, it would be to one who was sitting on a bag of gold."

"And he seems to have found her in the little Harmin. He has her around his thumb, and we can expect to hear wedding bells any day."

Sylvia smothered a gasp with both hands and finally stepped away from the flowers, lest they suspect her presence. How foolish she had been, thinking that the captain was merely paying her extravagant court as a matter of jest. If others had the same thought about their friendship as the two she had just overheard, no wonder Bennett Griffith considered she was making a fool of herself over the soldier!

She did not know whether she was more angry with Hugo Lannon for attempting to win her for the fortune he thought she had, or with Bennett Griffith, for believing she would take the man seriously.

How could she remain here, how could she face everyone, when she knew it would be impossible to control her feelings? What if Hugo had boasted of his conquest—as he saw it—to others besides the two she had overheard? Had she truly appeared so foolishly enchanted by his gallantry as to seem an easy prey?

She could see Hugo approaching for the dance he had been promised. But she knew she could not meet him now without showing what she thought of him for making her an object of public comment. Then she realized Bennett was standing not far away.

Had Bennett been near enough to the two gentlemen that he had heard them discussing Hugo's prospects with her? She hoped not, for it had seemed that he had recently been looking at her in a more favorable light than when they first met. If he thought, however, that she had been encouraging the captain to believe she would welcome marriage, his opinion of her would again be a poor one—and she felt she could not blame him for such thoughts.

At the moment, whatever Bennett might think of her, his presence was the less objectionable of the two. She sent him a beseeching look and he was at her side in an instant.

"Mr. Griffith, this is quite an imposition, I know, but I wish that I might ask a great favor of you."

Something had occurred to overset her, he realized. "Anything that I can do, Lady Harmin." At least, he thought, she turned to him in her trouble, whatever it might be, rather than to that officer who had been taking so much of her time. Somehow, he was happy that she had done so.

"As I said, it is an imposition, but I find that I am suffering from a severe migraine." This was the truth, for her head was beginning to throb in earnest from the knowledge that Hugo Lannon was boasting to his friends that he would marry her for her fortune. "I should not like, however, to take Charlotte away when she is enjoying herself so hugely." She could imagine the scene Charlotte might make if dragged away at this hour. "Would you be kind enough to escort her home after the ball?"

Although he had no idea what he had expected her

to say, her request was a surprise, and he hesitated for a moment. Misunderstanding the reason for his delay, Sylvia said, "Of course, I should have realized that this would be unfair to you, that you might have other plans for the remainder of the evening."

"Nothing of any import, I can assure you. Nothing that would prevent me—"

"There can be nothing wrong in your escorting her, sir, since you were a good friend of her father. I should not ask it of you otherwise."

"Almost as if I were an uncle," he said, smiling, and she forced a smile to match, although she had never felt less in the mood for levity.

"Exactly, sir. Will you do this for me, so that I may leave?"

Then, Captain Lannon seemed suddenly to appear at her side, saying, "This is our dance, I believe, my dear lady."

"You must forgive me, sir," she managed, unwilling to cause a scene here, "but I find myself extremely unwell and must leave at once."

It was unfortunate that she was leaving so soon, the captain reflected, but once they were alone in the carriage, he could declare himself. "Then you must permit me to see you home," he offered.

"That will be unnecessary, sir," Bennett Griffith announced with some force. "I have already told her ladyship that I shall see her safely home and then return to the ball to play escort to Lady Charlotte."

Captain Lannon seemed about to argue, unwilling to permit anyone but himself to shower her with attentions. He could discern, however, that the other man would not yield, and he turned away, clearly disappointed at the rebuff.

"That was kind of you, Mr. Griffith," Sylvia said, "to tell the gentleman that you had offered to see me home."

"I felt you did not wish his company."

"And you are correct." She wished she might never be forced to see the captain again. And what of the gentleman standing at her side? Why had she felt she could turn to him when she wished assistance? "But it is not at all necessary for you to accompany me, sir. If you will be kind enough to call my carriage . . ."

"Nonsense. There is no way I would let you go alone. It is clear that you are in no condition to do so. Wait here." He strode away, to return soon, her cloak over his arm. "I have sent a servant to bring your carriage around. Also, I made your regrets to Lady Melbourne, and she kindly has agreed to see to Charlotte until I can return for her."

"You are most kind," Sylvia murmured, placing her hand on his proffered arm, permitting him to lead her to the carriage. She wondered again if he had overheard the two gentlemen. Yet, if he had done so, he made no mention of the fact. Nor had he commented, as he had once done, upon Captain Lannon's unsuitability as a companion for her.

She knew now that he had been right in objecting to the captain, although her reason for disliking the man was not the same as his. Her migraine kept her from conversation, and the journey was made in silence until he handed her down from the carriage and accompanied her to the door.

When once more she thanked him for his kindness, he said briefly, "Not at all, Lady Harmin. It was a pleasure to have had the opportunity to serve you, although I regret the reason you needed my assistance. I trust you will feel more the thing by morning. And you need have no worry about Charlotte."

"In your company, Mr. Griffith, I do not," Sylvia said, barely able to speak for the pain which laced through her head. He turned away, and as the door closed behind him, she tottered and would have lost her balance had Porton not come quickly to her side.

"You are ill, milady," he said solicitously. "Shall I summon a physician?"

Sylvia shook her aching head. "No, if I can have a bit of rest, that is all I need." A bit of rest—and a chance to forget how Hugo had boasted to his friends that she would fall into his arms.

Sleep was long in coming while she examined her actions of the past days. It was true that she had enjoyed Captain Lannon's company and laughed at some of his outrageous remarks—perhaps had given him a bit more attention than was wise for one in her position. But had she truly behaved in such a way as to give him the right to think she would consider his suit? She did not think so.

Charlotte, on the other hand, felt that her evening had been a success. She was quite pleased at having had Bennett's escort from the ball—so pleased, in fact, that she unbent enough to enquire as to her stepmother's health. On being assured by Sylvia that she was feeling better, Charlotte told her that Lady Melbourne's two nieces had asked her to accompany them upon a shopping trip in Bond Street.

"That should be amusing for you; I think you might enjoy having company your own age," Sylvia told her. "You might even find some trifles to add to your wardrobe." She was happy to be left for a time, attempting to untangle her thoughts, to see if she was truly in any way to blame for the captain's behavior.

"You do not object if I go?" Charlotte asked, in apparent surprise, even though Sylvia had never opposed her friendship with other young ladies of the *ton*. "There will be the three of us, and, of course, we shall be accompanied by an abigail."

"I see no objection to your going." Sylvia knew her stepdaughter would be pleased to be going without her, but there was no reason why she should not be permitted this bit of freedom. The other young ladies would be well attended. Despite the gossip that the *ton* enjoyed whispering about Lady Melbourne's past indiscretions, she was known to be quite strict about members of her household.

Without other plans for the afternoon, when Charlotte had gone off with her friends, Sylvia took up a new copy of *Ackerman's Repository of Arts and Fashions*, and was studying some of the newer styles of gowns, wondering if Charlotte might wish to add several to her wardrobe. If Madame Celeste suggested that she should do so, of course; Charlotte would never take them if she thought the idea had come from Sylvia.

Porton coughed at the doorway to attract her attention, then announced that Captain Lannon was calling. "Please tell the captain that I am not at home," Sylvia said, aware that gentleman could hear her voice.

The captain flushed at the announcement, but persisted. "I wished to know if her ladyship had quite recovered from her indisposition."

"I could not say, sir," Porton told him stiffly. He did not understand whether the captain was suddenly no longer on her ladyship's list of favored callers, or whether this was a whim of the moment. However, as he often told himself, he had never pretended to be able to understand a lady's thinking, and it was not his place to determine the reasons for Lady Harmin's unusual behavior.

Captain Lannon frowned as he turned away from the house. Of course, Lady Harmin *had* appeared to be quite ill when she left the ball last evening. Doubtless that was the reason she had not accepted his escort from the ball. She would not wish him to see her at less than her best. If she felt no better today, it was probable that she might not wish to receive callers for the same reason. Her refusal to see him might be nothing more serious than that. Moreover, there was no reason to think she had singled him out for dismissal.

He would call again on the morrow. And this time he would put his fortune to the test with no more delay. No great need to beat about the bush when courting a widow. Indeed fortunate for him, as his creditors were beginning to turn nasty in their demands for payment. Harmin had been quite warm in the pocket, he had heard, so the lady should bring quite a dower with her.

When he called next afternoon, he distinctly heard the lady say, "I am not at home to Captain Lannon, Porton. Today, or in the future!"

Who did the lady think she was to treat him like this, blowing warm, then cold? He brushed past the irate butler to face her and demand, "Just what sort of game are you playing, Madam?"

"I am playing no games," Sylvia said icily. "It is merely that I think it would be best that you do not come here again." She crossed the room to the bell pull, but he was beside her before she could touch it, his hand tight about her wrist.

"By Heaven, you cannot do this to me," he said

angrily. "Have I ever said or done anything to make you think you can treat me—"

"I believe Lady Harmin asked you to leave." Bennett Griffith had come into the room—the second gentleman in a row to brush the butler from his path—when he heard the captain's angry tones upon entering the hall. "I suggest that you do so at once!"

Captain Lannon whirled about, still grasping Sylvia's wrist while glaring at the newcomer, uncertain as to the man's status in this household. Although her ladyship had several times insisted he was only her stepdaughter's friend, was he not the one to whom she had turned at the ball when she wished assistance? And apparently, he felt he had the right to enter unannounced.

It might be there was more than friendship between the two. Especially at this time, he could not admit to any rivals. "By what right do you think you can order me about?" the captain demanded.

"The right of any man who sees a lady being abused. You will release her ladyship at once—and take your leave." While you can still do so—the unspoken words hung in the air between them.

Looking from one to the other, Hugo Lannon sneered, "I did not know I was trespassing upon private property." He dropped Sylvia's wrist and took a step backward, daunted by the expression on the other man's face at the implication in his words. Porton had signaled to a footman, who held the door open for the departing officer.

"I—I thank you, sir," Sylvia managed to say, although she wondered how it happened that he had come at such an opportune moment.

"It was nothing, Lady Harmin."

Brown eyes and violet eyes gazed into each other, almost without their volition, the two moved closer . . .

In the doorway, Porton coughed discreetly and announced, "A lady and gentleman to see you, milady. He says that he is Lord Harmin."

# CHAPTER
## ❧ 7 ❧

Sylvia gasped as she stepped quickly away from Bennett. "Lord—" But Martin could not be here, she thought; he had been dead more than a year and a half, and it was improbable that his spirit could be wandering about. Suddenly she felt foolish as she recalled that this was of course the new earl. Martin's cousin. She had forgot about him since she came to London; in fact, she had never received any information that he had returned to England. Resolutely, Sylvia now replied, "Show the lady and gentleman in at once, Porton."

The tall, spare, man who was ushered into the room bore no resemblance to Martin's comfortable bulk, but he was well matched by the dour, spinsterish lady who preceded him. Her face, however, was quite pale, in contrast to the browned skin which told of the earl's stay in a warmer, sunnier clime.

71

Bennett retreated as Sylvia advanced to meet the newcomers. "Lord Harmin, it is good of you to call. I did not know that you had returned from your trip abroad. And—Lady Harmin?"

"Not yet," the earl said with a laugh that barely escaped being a whinny. "But soon, I am happy to say, now that I am through with my wandering. I intend to remain in England. My adventures in Jamaica were interesting enough, when I was not encumbered by a title and estates. But now I am content to settle down and take over my duties here. May I present Miss Hodges, my future countess? My dear Godiva, this is my late cousin's widow."

Godiva! Sylvia bit her lip to prevent a giggle, for the name conjured a voluptuous female, one totally unlike the newcomer. Regaining her control, she said, "You are most welcome, Miss Hodges. May I wish both of you happy?"

"Thank you." The lady's voice was as austere as was her appearance. She was clearly several years older than her future husband, Sylvia thought, two or three years past her thirtieth birthday. And when she spoke, she showed an even wider expanse of tooth and gum than did her intended, a feat Sylvia would have thought impossible. "I must say that I am quite surprised to find that you are not in mourning, Lady Harmin." Her tone was one of deep censure, although Sylvia wondered why the stranger took it upon herself to judge another's behavior.

"As are any number of other people, I do not doubt, Miss Hodges," she replied, determined to keep her temper. After all, the lady was a guest. At least, she was the earl's guest. "But I thought it the wisest thing to put aside my mourning when I arranged my stepdaughter's come-out, so that I would not put a blight upon the occasion. Miss Hodges—Wyndham"—that was his name, was it not? for she could scarcely bring herself to continue calling the new earl "Harmin"—"May I present Mr. Bennett Griffith? He will be a neighbor of yours when you have settled in your estate."

The earl nodded in Bennett's direction, but made no other acknowledgment. "Yes," he said instead, "you were speaking about your bringing out Lady Charlotte. That is our reason for calling upon you. At least, one of the reasons. As head of your family—"

"My husband left the guardianship of his daughter to me, sir," Sylvia told him firmly. "And of course, you were not present to be consulted." Not that Martin would have wanted his cousin to have the management of his daughter, had the man been available. Sylvia had known his wishes, and he had been confident that she would obey them.

"Very shortsighted of him," Miss Hodges said, before her intended could speak.

"Not at all. My husband was in full control of his faculties and was aware he was dying. He also knew I would be able to see to his daughter's future."

"But to give a female—and so young a female—control of so much money. Money that should properly have been a part of Harmin's estate . . ."

"You are quite mistaken about that, Miss Hodges." And why should the lady take it upon herself to lecture about such matters, when she was not yet married to the earl? Did she think him incapable of speaking for himself? Or was it merely that she must have the final word on every subject? "Both Charlotte's inheritance and my own allowance are paid from Lord Harmin's—my late husband's—unentailed property. Property which came to him from his mother's family, and which he always kept apart from the estate income."

"But this house—"

"—Is part of the entail, of course. It was never our intention to remain here after the end of the Season. Do you wish to take possession of it at once?" Pointedly ignoring the lady, who appeared determined to be insulting as well as to control the conversation, Sylvia addressed her question to the earl.

Lord Harmin hesitated, as if in an attempt to decide. "No, I think it would be satisfactory for you to remain here for the balance of the Season. The time is so short. However—"

"However," his intended said firmly, once more taking the reins of the conversation into her hands, "you must know there is a great deal to be done both to this place and to the manor house to modernize them. We can begin work at the manor, I suppose, and allow the renovation of this place to wait—for a time."

Sylvia thought of the comfortable old manor house to which Martin had taken her. It was true that certain of the carpets and draperies should be replaced, but she had not thought too much else needed to be done. As for this house, although it had been more than five years since Martin had refurbished it for her, everything was almost sparkling new. What did the lady have in mind for its "renovation"? Was Godiva a devotee of the current, but to Sylvia's mind, most unattractive craze for sofas with crocodile legs and sphinxes decorating every possible spot?

She smothered a sigh, thinking of the lovely rosewood furniture which would doubtless be relegated to the attic when the redoubtable Godiva took charge. Either that, she thought, or covered with silver or gilt paint, as so many families were doing now. And what of the linenfold panels and the walls which had been copied from Adam's designs? What would happen to them? Still, both this and the manor house would soon be Godiva's homes to do with as she wished.

"Thank you for permitting us to use the house for the next weeks. After all, as you say, it will not be long."

The long-faced Lord Harmin permitted himself a near-smile, one which exposed no more than half his teeth. "I hope you do not think I would be so ungenerous as to order you out with no opportunity to make other arrangements. I do think, however, that it might have been better had you delayed my cousin's come-out for another season."

"But Charlotte is already seventeen—"

"Still a child. Had you waited until next year, until I had married, then my lady could have presided over matters instead." The clear implication was that his lady would have handled matters far better than Sylvia was doing. However, on this occasion, it appeared that he had spoken without consulting the lady in question.

"On the contrary," Miss Hodges said emphatically, "I am certain that the dowager is quite able to see to the girl's needs. After all, she has known her for some years. For my part, I think I shall be quite occupied with other things, with no time for such trifles."

"Perhaps you are right—certainly, you are. The frivolities of a London Season are not for us." He spoke with a touch of sadness, as if *he* might have welcomed some of the frivolities.

The lady nodded, content that the earl agreed with her pronouncement, as Sylvia noted he customarily did. She could not suppress a brief stab of pity for the earl; it was evident that he would be—indeed, he already was—

beneath the cat's foot. "I am sorry that Charlotte is not here to meet you," she said. "She is shopping with some friends. Had we known of your visit, she could easily have postponed her errand."

"No matter," Miss Hodges stated flatly. "I find that I am not entirely in sympathy with the over-exuberance of the very young. And there is another matter of some importance about which we wished to speak. Harmin—"

"Of course, I had not forgot, my dear. It has been brought to my . . . to our attention that, when the Season is ended, you are planning to remove from the manor to the Dower House."

"Yes, that was Martin's wish for us. He thought you would have no objection to our remaining there until Charlotte is married. After that, I should make other arrangements, of course."

"It is understandable that the late Lord Harmin would wish for his wife and daughter to remain on the estate. And if I were not to be married soon, the arrangement would be quite satisfactory. As it is—"

"Stop beating about the bush, Harmin. What the earl is attempting to say, Lady Harmin, is that neither my mother nor my Aunt Esmerelda are in good health, and I wish to have them near me."

"I am sorry to hear of their ill health." Sylvia hoped the slight tremor in her voice would be taken as a sign of her concern, rather than as an attempt to hide the mirth which would be quite inappropriate for the occasion. "But I suppose that means—"

"—That, when the Season is over, we must suggest that you and your stepdaughter make other arrangements."

Sylvia opened her mouth to protest, but looking from the determined face of the bride-to-be to the almost shamefaced earl, she realized it would useless to do so. "Certainly," she said at last. "It may take us several weeks to find suitable lodgings, but I can assure you we shall leave as soon as we can make proper arrangements."

Bennett, who had retired to the windowseat after his near dismissal by the earl, and who had been watching in admiration as the young countess dealt with the ruthless Miss Hodges and her too-obedient swain, now came forward. "There will be no problem at all, Lord Harmin," he said smoothly. "I shall be more than happy to provide shelter for Lady Harmin and Lady Charlotte."

"But—" Lord Harmin's laugh was definitely a whinny now. "But you are an unmarried man, I understand, Griffith. It would be most improper for my cousin and Lady Harmin to reside with you. As head of the family—"

"Oh, I did not mean that they should stay with *me*. I have a small estate in Kent, which I seldom visit. It was my plan to offer it to the ladies. They could stay there with complete propriety."

The earl hesitated; the offer would take the widow and her stepdaughter off his property and, he supposed, off his hands as well, assuring him of peace in his own home. Still, he could not prevent himself from wondering what the *ton*—which he could not despise as much as his betrothed appeared to do—would say to his agreeing to such an arrangement.

As if he knew what must be going through the other man's mind, Bennett continued, "After all, my father was one of the late Lord Harmin's closest friends. I could do no less for his wife and his daughter than to permit them to stay on one of my estates."

"*I* see nothing improper about it," Godiva Hodges stated, with a firmness that dared any of those present to contradict her. The sooner the interlopers—as she now considered them—were gone, the better it would be. Under her stare, the earl finally nodded.

"Perhaps that might be the best way," he owned.

"Thank you, gentlemen," Sylvia put in, again ignoring the lady's fiat in the matter, "but neither of you has asked me what I think about being handed over to the care of Mr. Griffith. Allowing us to move to any of his estates is an imposition upon him."

"Not at all, Lady Harmin," Bennett replied. "The place is untenanted, save for a few servants. It is not too far from London for you to come to the city when you like—and if it does not suit, you can make other arrangements whenever you wish to do so. However, I assure you that you would be doing me a favor if you agreed to go there." He realized, almost with a start, that he meant the words; nothing would give him greater pleasure than to see that proper provision was made for Sylvia . . . for Charlotte, as well, he added mentally.

"Very well, sir, if it is agreeable with Charlotte, we shall accept."

"Why should it matter what the child may wish?" Miss Hodges wished to know. "Merely tell her what you plan to do. She must obey you."

Sylvia laughed. "It is clear, Miss Hodges, that you do not know my stepdaughter." She thought it would do the forceful Miss Hodges a great deal of good to have to handle Charlotte for a time. Then she would have had no doubt the girl could care for herself quite well, despite any effort on the part of the countess-to-be. Still, she would not wish such a fate on Charlotte. "She has a will of her own, has she not, Ben . . . Mr. Griffith?"

"She has, indeed. However, I do not foresee any reason for her not to like the move. There will be friends who will be spending the summer in the area, so she will not lack for companionship."

"Under those circumstances, we shall accept your offer with thanks."

"Then it is arranged," the earl said thankfully. "You know, of course, Lady Harmin, that when my dear Godiva and I are wed and settled on the estate you and Charlotte will be welcome to visit us whenever you choose. We wish you to look upon it as your home still."

The look on his lady's face told her opinion of such an invitation, but she said nothing. Sylvia did not doubt that, once they were alone, however, she would make the gentleman rue his impetuousness in issuing it. It did not matter to her. She would prefer *not* to see the changes the new countess would make in her former home.

Having accomplished their aims, the couple prepared to take their leave. Porton, having announced the visitors, had not awaited his mistress's order, but had immediately ordered tea to be served. Followed by a footman and two maids, he came into the room, saying, "Your tea, milady."

"Th–thank you, Porton," Sylvia said. "Will you have tea, Miss Hodges and—"

"No, we must go. There is much to do." The lady gave her husband-to-be a look that ordered him to agree with her.

"Then you may leave everything, Porton. Mr. Griffith and I shall have tea. Should you be in London in the next several weeks"—once more she ignored the lady and addressed herself to the earl—"we shall be happy to see you again. I know that Charlotte would like to meet you as well."

The earl muttered something unintelligible and followed the lady out of the room. As the door closed behind them, Sylvia and Bennett looked at one another, then he said, "It is clear who will be ruling *that* household, is it not?"

Sylvia nodded. "And while I cannot fail to deplore his being so different from Martin in every way, I can only pity him—although I suppose he must be happy enough. But do you know"—she had been struck by a sudden thought—"when that dreadful woman— who must be eight or nine years older than myself— when she marries the earl, I *shall* be the dowager countess."

"And the new countess will be Godiva." He chuckled. "If she were to ride about the countryside as her namesake was supposed to have done, would there be any danger of a Peeping Tom?"

"I doubt it. What names. Godiva—and Esmerelda."

Laughing until her sides ached, she collapsed against him, aware that he was as overcome as she with the mirth they had been controlling. But as his arms closed about her, Sylvia was also aware of a strange, warm feeling deep within her, something quite unknown to her, but something quite wonderful.

"I . . . I must thank you once more for coming to my aid," she managed to say. "And for the second time today."

"You know that you can command me at any time, my lady." Then, with an effort, as he remembered who this lady was, Bennett stepped backward and shook his head, as if to free himself from the emotion which had nearly overpowered him. It had felt so natural to hold her; in another instant, he would have kissed her. How had this situation come about?

"You must recall that I warned you against Lannon." His voice was harsher than usual as he attempted to control his thoughts.

Sylvia recoiled as if she had been slapped. "So you did, sir." Ice appeared to drip from every word.

"I . . . I have overstayed my visit. I merely called to see if Charlotte would like a drive in the Park this afternoon," he prevaricated, wondering if his words sounded as lame to her as to himself. Why could he not say that he had been worried about her? He had forced himself to stay away yesterday, but could do so no longer.

"I regret that you are too late. Charlotte has already gone on a shopping trip—with friends of whom I am certain *you* would approve."

"In that case, I shall call again. I am happy that I could be of service to you, Lady Harmin." He bowed over the hand she mutely extended, brushing it with his lips, steeling himself against a wish to make the caress an ardent one.

# CHAPTER

## ❧ 8 ❧

A moment later, Bennett had retrieved his hat from the butler and seemed suddenly to find himself upon the street, still wondering what had happened. Twice during his short stay this afternoon, he had caught himself upon the verge of taking Sylvia in his arms. The last time, he had actually done so—and even if they were laughing together at the time over the new earl and his formidable but misnamed intended, embracing Sylvia was an unforgivable act. What might she think of him for behaving in such a way?

Sylvia stood where he had left her, the fingers of her other hand touching the spot his lips had caressed. Bennett was quite the most exasperating man she had ever known, she told herself. He had come to her rescue the night of Lady Melbourne's ball and again today by sending Captain Lannon away.

Then he had offered refuge to her and Charlotte after the new earl had told them they would not be welcome to return to the Dower House at the end of the Season. The two of them had clung to one another when the earl and his betrothed had gone, laughing over the improbable pair—and for a breathtaking moment, Sylvia had thought he was about to kiss her. Instead, he had drawn away from her, reminding her, almost coldly, of the first part of his visit and holding her to blame for Hugo Lannon's behavior toward her, implying that she had encouraged the man's attention.

She knew it had not been her intention to encourage Hugo, but it seemed the officer must have been emboldened by the fact she had found him amusing, must have considered her amusement a sign her interest in him was far greater than it actually was.

There was nothing wrong, she supposed, in Hugo's having leaped to such a conclusion about her feelings, erroneous though it had been. If he had continued his courtship in the manner in which he had approached her, she *might* have been tempted to consider his suit, although she was able to tell herself now that she would never seriously have done so. Still, to have crowed to his friends over what he supposed to be the ease of his conquest of her, as he had done—she could never forgive that.

"I could have rid myself of him quite easily today," she murmured. "All I needed to do was to say four words. 'I have no money.' He would have vanished at once, without making a scene."

Perhaps, she thought, her reason for not telling him the truth about her financial situation was a petty one, but Sylvia told herself she had sufficient provocation for treating him as she had done.

"Still," she soliloquized, "it ought to be a lady's choice whether or not she wishes to receive a gentleman's attentions; it ought not be necessary to explain to him why she wishes to put an end to those attentions. Hugo insulted me by boasting to his friends that I was an easy conquest; he did not deserve that I should give him a reason for wishing to break off our acquaintance."

Yet she was aware that had she explained matters to the captain, there would have been no reason for Bennett Griffith to come to her rescue as he had done today. She felt her heart beating faster when she recalled that moment after Hugo had left, when she and Bennett had stood so near to one another, their gazes seemingly attempting to read each other's souls. The feeling when he held her so briefly in his arms, however, had been nearly enough to suffocate her. Had he known similar feelings?

What would she have done if he had attempted to kiss her? Would she have slapped him for his effrontery? Would she have retreated in icy indignation and ordered him to leave the house? Or, she wondered, would she have found the sensation pleasurable?

Her only experience with kisses had been with Martin's infrequent, almost dutiful efforts, and although she had accepted them in the same spirit they were given, she was now forced to own that they had aroused no true emotion in her. Nor had she ever been tempted to engage in a dalliance—until now.

She quickly pushed that thought aside, reminding herself that the gentleman *might* have been tempted for an instant, but that was merely because they had been standing so close to one another. Doubtless he would have behaved in the same way with any other lady of his acquaintance. Indeed, if she had been some other lady, it was far more probable that he *would* have kissed her.

The incident had meant nothing to her, she attempted to convince herself. And certainly it could have meant nothing to him. He truly distrusted her, and made it clear that he had called at the house today only to check upon Charlotte's welfare.

The fact that Bennett had once—no, twice—more come to her assistance was beside the point. All she wanted was to see the girl safely launched into the *ton* and, in time, to find her a suitable husband.

That *was* all, was it not?

She had made no plans for her own future. Her marriage—aside from Charlotte's enmity—had been pleasant enough, but had aroused in her no desire to seek a second husband. The allowance left her by Martin was enough to keep her in some comfort, if not in luxury.

She supposed that she would find a companion and settle down near enough to London that she might visit the museums, perhaps the theatre as well—although she might need an escort for such visits. It should not be too difficult to find one among her friends who was willing to see her about from time to time, someone who would expect nothing more than friendship.

She would also be able to pay occasional visits to her dressmaker, although she doubted that she would employ Madame Celeste after she had found Charlotte a husband. Nor would she need to have a new gown for every occasion. At present, it was necessary for her to be as well dressed as her stepdaughter, but a couturière of Madame's reputation was an extravagance for a lady who would have a somewhat limited income. All of this must lie several years in the future, however, and need not concern her now.

Sylvia was not certain why she was beginning to think about her own future. Doubtless, it was because of Bennett's offer to permit the two of them to reside on his estate in Kent. She supposed that it would be proper for them to do so until they could make other arrangements or until Charlotte had found a suitable husband. Even the censorious Miss Hodges had not disapproved of their going there.

After Charlotte married, of course, it would be quite impossible for Sylvia to remain there alone. For that matter, she doubted that she would be welcome on his property when her stepdaughter had gone.

She reminded herself once more that it was much too early for her to concern herself about such matters. It was Charlotte's future which was important at the present. Her own plans could wait.

From time to time, she saw Hugo Lannon at various affairs. But after she had twice refused to dance with him, Sylvia was pleased to observe that he did not approach her again. On occasion, when she was aware of the pained looks he cast in her direction, she felt that she ought to have given him an explanation for her conduct.

Then she would remember that he had bandied her name about in public—if not to everyone, at least to some of his friends—as if she were a . . . a . . . "No," she told herself firmly. "If he is suffering—which I doubt, unless he regrets the loss of the fortune he thought I have—he deserves to do so."

The daily offering of flowers continued to arrive from Bennett Griffith. Although she reminded herself that she should still be angry with him for the things he had said to her from time to time, she was forced to own to herself that he had been kind to her on occasion. Also, he never failed to ask her to stand up with him for a dance, sometimes two, and she was certain there was no better dancer in all of London. She always agreed to the dances, but she sometimes wondered if he shared her feelings when the dance brought them together.

Whenever she and Charlotte rode together in the Park, he was certain to join them. And Sylvia noted that, although he appeared to give the greater part of his attention to her stepdaughter, Bennett never omitted an opportunity to draw her into the talk, despite Charlotte's efforts to persuade him to ignore her.

Sylvia wondered if she was succeeding in her original plan to bring the gentleman to her feet, or if he continued to consider her a bad influence upon Charlotte. Whatever his reason, she found herself absurdly pleased whenever he sought her out. Her thought of casting him aside once she had won his attention no longer seemed important to her. In fact, she owned to herself that she would have preferred a much closer association with him— then faced the chilling thought that such an association was not to be expected.

One evening, he arrived at Madame Lefebre's ball— by accident, she told herself—though Sylvia had mentioned that she and Charlotte would be attending. On this occasion, he was accompanied by a gentleman who was possibly ten years younger but who appeared to be much the same type as he. Sylvia noticed that Bennett introduced the other man to people he passed but continued directly toward the place where she was seated.

"Lady Harmin," he said, "may I present my young friend, Colin Waite, newly up from the country?"

Sylvia murmured a greeting, extending her hand. Mr. Waite made a creditable bow, then spoiled his attempt to appear a man-about-town by turning to Bennett, saying, "Must you say *that* whenever you present me to someone? It makes me sound the veriest clodpoll."

"Not at all, sir," Sylvia told him with a laugh. "We ourselves have only recently come from the country, my stepdaughter and I. And we think we are—what is the expression?—awake on every suit."

Bennett's roar of laughter caused heads to turn in their direction. Mr. Waite looked a bit startled, then joined the laughter.

Charlotte's most recent partner was returning her after their dance. Despite her dislike of appearing in her stepmother's company, the girl realized she must make this concession to the rules of the *ton*. She frowned slightly when she saw the young gentleman conversing with Sylvia, but smiled upon him when he was introduced to her as Bennett's friend.

Apparently dazzled by her smile, the young man bowed even more deeply to Charlotte and requested the favor of a dance.

"Well, I had *almost* promised this one to Mr. Alvin," she said, smiling at him once more. "But since you are a newcomer, I am certain he will understand if I dance with you instead."

"I cannot believe anyone would understand missing the opportunity to dance with you, Lady Charlotte! But I shall not wait about to argue the question with him." He offered his arm and led Charlotte to the floor.

Sylvia recalled that she had not yet told Charlotte about Bennett's offer to allow them to stay on his estate in Kent. When she considered the way she was beginning to feel about the gentleman, she was not certain it was a good idea to take advantage of his kindness in the matter. Until she could make better arrangements,

however, she was grateful to him for such consideration—even though she suspected he had been thinking
mainly of Charlotte's welfare, and possibly considering
that he could keep his eye upon her better if she were
close at hand.

Time enough to tell the girl about the idea when the
Season was ended. Or might it be better if Bennett himself were to do so? Charlotte would take the suggestion
more readily if it came from him. At present, Sylvia was
content merely to have the gentleman at her side.

"For someone who is so newly come to the city, your
young friend seems to have no trouble in accustoming
himself to our ways," she commented, laughing again
as she looked from the rapidly retreating couple to the
disappointed face of young Mr. Alvin, who had arrived
upon the scene too late to insist upon his dance.

"Yes, I must say that he has always been quick to
adapt himself to his surroundings," Bennett replied. "As
you put it—'awake on every suit.' "

Sylvia placed her hand over her mouth to stifle a laugh
as she said, "That was dreadful of me, was it not? I fear
I must have overheard some of Charlotte's young friends
say that."

"It was only surprising to hear you using a cant term."
He looked down at her questioningly, and Sylvia indicated the chair at her side, somehow inexplicably pleased
when he accepted the invitation. Was she always to feel
this way when he came near? If so, how could she bear
to live in his home, even if he did not come to that
particular estate? Just the knowledge that the place was
his . . .

"I must say, sir," she improvised quickly, "that I was
rather surprised to see you bear-leading the young man.
That is what it is called, is it not?"

He grinned at her, but shook his head. "That is not exactly what I am doing—although, I suppose, in a way you are correct. I am showing him about London, so perhaps one might consider me a tutor—of sorts. Colin is a neighbor's son; he has been completely army-mad since he was a child . . . will not listen when I try to tell him there is less glory than drudgery in the life. His father thinks he should have a bit of town bronze, and Colin has agreed to spend a few weeks in the city, if, in return, I will speak to his father about purchasing him a commission."

"And shall you do so?"

"Of course, although I have not yet decided what I shall say. Naturally, Colin hopes that I will speak in favor of having a commission purchased for him, while his father and I hope the lure of the *ton* will turn his thoughts in another direction."

"I find it difficult to understand why anyone should wish to enter the army, but it seems many young men aspire to do so."

Recalling how quickly the lady had leaped into the fray when she saw the ruffian mistreating a boy, Bennett suppressed a smile. "Oh, I can understand his wish very well. I felt the same when I was his age. Experience taught me the folly of my thoughts."

"Oh yes, I recall Lady Sefton saying that you had been wounded." Dared she ask if he had received that tiny scar at the same time? No, it was best not to do so.

"It was nothing worth the mentioning, a mere scratch. But her ladyship likes to make a great deal of it. And it was not at Talveras, but at Cuidad Rodrigo—which I suppose is more difficult for her to remember."

"You did not correct her?" How could she remember that about him? But then, did she not recall everything he had said or done, whether it was a compliment or a complaint, or even when it had nothing to do with her at all? Merely the fact that *he* was involved was enough to impress it upon her memory.

"No, there was no reason why I should do so. She was so happy at what she *thought* was the right battle. And how could I bear to contradict a lady?" As he said that, he hoped the lady before him did not remember that he had contradicted *her* on several occasions.

The lady recalled the occasions quite well, but did not wish to spoil the moment by referring to them. "But, I remember, she said at Charlotte's ball that you should be wearing a sling. Does your arm pain you?"

"At times, of course, as I am told old wounds often do. Doubtless, it is a sign of advancing age, but it is certainly not worth the mentioning. Can we not find something more interesting to talk about? I am certain ladies do not care to hear of wars."

"N–no." It made no sense, but she found that she did want to know what had happened, to know everything about the gentleman. Not necessarily about his war experience, but what he had done as a younger man, as a child, what he wanted of life. Everything about him, in fact. But she must not hint of such things. "Nor about any sort of violence, of course. You must think us quite frivolous."

"Sometime, Lady Harmin," he said in a low tone, "I should like to tell you exactly what I think of you."

The memory of what he had said about her several times washed over her like an icy flood. "I believe I already know your opinion of me," she said shortly.

"But—"

They were interrupted by the arrival of Colin Waite with Charlotte on his arm. They had not realized that the dance had ended until the young man spoke. "I merely wished to say, Bennett, that I do not think there is any hurry in speaking to my father about the commission. I may not wish it, after all."

Bennett and Sylvia stared at his beaming face, neither able to say a word as the younger pair moved off, Colin having received permission to take Charlotte down to supper.

# CHAPTER
## 9

It had not been her intention to marry off her step-daughter this Season. Sylvia had hoped that Charlotte would form some lasting friendships, possibly one or more that might blossom into romance in a year or two. If they did not, there was time for Charlotte to meet numbers of other people. She was merely carrying out the promise she had made to Martin that she would bring the girl out properly. After all, Charlotte was still so very young . . . much too young to think of marriage.

Of course, *she* had been only seventeen when she became Martin's wife, but that was a different matter. Or was it so different, after all? At any rate, although her own marriage had been satisfactory enough in many ways, it had not been a love match. She wanted something more than mere contentment for Charlotte. Something that would stir her blood, something Sylvia felt had been lacking in her own marriage. She would not own, even to herself, that she had felt more warmth in that moment when Bennett had held her than in all her years with Martin.

She had no intention of match-making—as she knew many of the hopeful mamas were doing—but if Charlotte *should* be fortunate enough to find that all-important person this Season, Sylvia would be only too happy for her, despite the girl's youth. However, clearly it would have to be a gentleman better than most she was meeting now, for it seemed to her stepmother that far too many were only pleasure seekers.

There must be someone better, perhaps someone like young Mr. Waite, Sylvia thought. That gentleman was of a good family, although without title, and she did not doubt he would prove steady enough once he had put the idea of a commission firmly out of his mind.

As his father and Bennett had hoped, the idea of army life appeared to be less important to the young man since his arrival in London. He was handsome enough that any number of young ladies were hoping he would throw his handkerchief in their direction, but he apparently had eyes for no one except Charlotte.

It was clear enough the young man was smitten from the moment he had been presented to the girl, but she did not seem to return his regard. She danced with him on several occasions, but gave him no more of her time than any other young gentleman. In fact, there were several others who appeared to claim more of her interest.

"Why is it, do you suppose?" Bennett asked in a low tone, watching the two. He had gravitated to Sylvia's side, as he often did at these affairs. "I had thought the pair of them would suit admirably."

Sylvia shrugged. "One can never tell about these things, you know. Despite our best wishes, we cannot pick another's friends." Actually, she thought she knew the answer to the problem. Charlotte apparently sensed that her stepmother approved of the young man—and if Sylvia liked him, Charlotte would never permit herself to show an interest in him, no matter what her private feelings might be. Her antagonism toward her stepmother had not been changed by the admiration she received from others.

"Charlotte could easily make a worse choice than your young friend, I am certain," she said, looking toward the pair, regretting that she had made her own liking for the young man so clear that Charlotte could not fail to see it—and resent it, of course. She should have been wise enough to conceal her feelings, but that had always been difficult for Sylvia to do.

While her stepmother watched, Charlotte shook her head in answer to Colin's request for a dance and went off on the arm of Graham Floyd. Sylvia sighed. Indeed, she could make a worse choice, and was apparently doing so. This was entirely the *wrong* sort of gentleman for Charlotte.

"You do not approve of him?" Bennett asked.

Sylvia looked at Bennett, surprised that he seemed to have sensed her thoughts. In fact, she had forgot for the moment that he was still at her side—and then wondered how she could have done so, even while she worried about her stepdaughter. It was true that the gentlemen now spent more time near her than he had before—but, far from disapproving of his being there, she had begun to welcome the thought that he wanted to be near her.

The change in her feelings was something quite beyond her understanding. For all she could tell, Bennett Griffith was as much her foe as he had been at the beginning, and only stayed near her in an effort to find something about her conduct that he might criticize.

Then she realized that it had been some days since he had made any complaint about her behavior. Was the gentleman, perhaps, becoming . . . somewhat interested? She would not permit herself to think his feelings were deeper than that, but *could* he have felt something of what she had felt during their brief embrace?

Her earlier plan to bring him to her feet and then to dismiss him had long been put aside, for some reason that she could not explain to herself. Or at least she did not *wish* to explain it. Yet, there were barriers between them that he had been the one to set up—any number of reasons why there could never be anything beyond the faintest friendship between herself and Bennett Griffith.

If she could expect even as much as friendship. Despite the change in his attitude toward her these past days, she still felt that Bennett—how easy it had become in her own mind to call him by his first name, and she now sometimes caught herself addressing him in that way—still appeared to think it possible that she was mistreating her stepdaughter in some unnamed way. Doubtless, he had reached that conclusion after listening to Charlotte's tales.

Still, she reminded herself, he had clearly felt that way about her before they met, so his disapprobation could not have been entirely due to anything Charlotte might have said regarding her stepmother.

He was looking at her questioningly, and she realized that, wrapped once more in her own thoughts about him—as were so many of her thoughts these days— she had not answered. "No," she said, "I do not like the notion of Charlotte's interest in Mr. Floyd. This is one time when I wish I might influence her in her choice of companions. But I fear any attempt on my part would drive her even closer to him."

"He appears to be well accepted by everyone." Bennett told himself that doubtless *he* was prejudiced against the fellow because of his dandified appearance. He was pleased to know that the lady seemed to share his dislike of the young man, although he doubted her reason was the same as his. Ladies did not appear to think there was anything amiss in a gentleman's foppishness.

"He may be accepted by some people, perhaps," Sylvia said, shaking her head, "but that is definitely not so as far as everyone is concerned, from what I have been told. His grandfather is a viscount, which doubtless counts for a great deal with many of the *ton*, even though he is the son of a younger son. The merest hint of relationship to a title is enough to impress many."

"You are right."

His dry tone reminded Sylvia that this gentleman had once thought Martin's title—and his wealth—had been instrumental in her acceptance of the early offer. Perhaps those attributes had done so in her parents' eyes, but it had been Martin's kindness to her from the moment they met that had meant so much more than any material advantages he could offer.

It was something many people could not have understood. Growing up as she had done, with parents who had left her to the care of unfeeling servants until it was time to pitch her into the *ton* to make an advantageous marriage, she had clung instinctively to this gentleman who had always treated her like a princess—or as she had supposed a princess would be treated.

Martin's kindness to her had endured throughout their marriage, and there had been only the slightest hint of disappointment that she had not been able to give him the heir he wanted. Nor had he held her to blame for the lack, as many husbands would have done, knowing that she was as unhappy as he about the matter.

Once more she had gone off into her memories of the past, forgetting about the gentleman at her side until he drew her back to the present by saying, "Then it cannot be his ancestry which makes you dislike Floyd."

Once or twice, she reminded herself, she had felt the same sort of kindness from Bennett that Martin had shown her. At the moment, it seemed he shared her feelings, at least to an extent. It might be, she warned herself, that he shared only her concern for Charlotte. "No, I do not believe that lineage is important, as long as the gentleman comes from honest stock. Rather, it is some of the tales I have heard of this particular gentleman's habits that worry me. He seems to be a wild sort."

"Many young men are like that. Wisdom usually comes with maturity."

Sylvia shook her head. "No, I do not mean the wild spirits one thinks of in young gentlemen. There are rumors of . . . of other things." The whispers she had heard were not the sort of matters about which one could speak to a gentleman, even if he were closer than Bennett Griffith might be. But they were definitely things which would prevent his being a proper companion for Charlotte.

However, it appeared that, once more, Bennett had read her thoughts. "From your tone, I sense they are not the interests that one would approve. Would you like for me to speak to Charlotte about him?"

"Do you think it would be of help if you did so?" she asked. "I should like to put a stop to the association, but I know all too well that Charlotte would not accept any advice from me."

He wondered if he had detected a hint of bitterness in her remark. She had said that any attempt on her part to influence her stepdaughter would send her in the opposite direction. And now this. Could it be that the lady was jealous of her stepdaughter's popularity? Still, she herself seemed to attract her share of attention—more than was customarily given to one in her position—so he doubted that was her reason. "I can see what I might do. If nothing else works, I might be able to warn the young man away."

"You are being most kind." Sylvia placed her hand on his arm, withdrawing it immediately as he glanced at it. She did not know what had urged her to touch him; she only knew she had wanted to do so.

Perplexed by her feelings, quite different from anything she had known, she said quickly, "I am certain that you can understand . . . it is so important that Charlotte's first Season should be a success. I should not wish for anything to happen to cause unpleasant talk, and I cannot avoid the feeling that her association with young Mr. Floyd would do so sooner or later."

"You need not worry." If she had not removed her hand from his sleeve so abruptly, he would have placed his own over hers. He would have done that merely as a gesture of reassurance, he told himself. What other reason could he have for wishing to touch her? In confusion, he continued, "I wish for young Charlotte's success as much as you."

In truth, he thought Sylvia—Lady Harmin, he reminded himself—might well be overcautious in her protection of her stepdaughter. If what she had in mind for her was truly protection, and not merely a wish to keep the girl firmly under her thumb.

However, if the latter were true, would she have brought Charlotte to London and presented her to the *ton* rather than keeping her at home, where she would truly have been in control of Charlotte's fortune? Of course, he told himself, she could scarcely have done that, since the new earl was eager to take possession of his estate— then recalled that she had not expected the heir to return so soon. It might well have been several more years before the earl came home—and Sylvia would have been able to rule the girl as she liked with interference from no one.

It was probable that she, indeed, spoke only out of her concern for Charlotte's welfare. Bennett remembered her kindness to the serving maid; was it not credible that she would care even more deeply for her husband's daughter?

While Sylvia and Bennett were discussing Charlotte's friendship with Mr. Floyd, that young lady was dancing with the gentleman and frankly enjoying a flirtation with him. He was quite different from most of the young gentlemen of the *ton*; his compliments often bordered on the scandalous and his dancing surpassed that of his contemporaries. Something about him gave Charlotte a feeling that she was dallying with something almost dangerous—a feeling she had never before known.

A couple passed them, and Charlotte gasped at the sight of Caroline Lamb. Determined as always to shock the *ton*, that lady was clad in a gown of brilliant scarlet— a color many of the gossips declared was well suited to her activities. The gown, moreover, was cut so daringly low that Charlotte wondered how she could keep from bursting out over the top of it and—in defiance of present fashion—so tightly fitted to her form that she could barely move.

Hearing his partner's gasp, Graham Floyd slanted an amused look at her. "I should like very much to see you in such a gown."

"I . . . like that?" Charlotte could scarcely take her eyes from the clusters of gems that made up the greater part of the lady's bodice. Surely they must be paste; would she flaunt a fortune in rubies? Then the full force of his words struck her. "But . . . but . . ." she stammered, wondering if he could truly be serious about wishing to see her like *that*. "But I—I must wear white." It was the first excuse that came to her mind.

The young man turned to study her carefully. "Yes, but such a gown as that, even if made up in white, would suit you quite well. Nothing like the child's gowns you are forced to wear now."

He was thinking of the rakish friends before whom he would enjoy displaying the young lady in such a gown—and also how easily he might divest her of it. For a young lady who would dare to appear in public clad in such a fashion could not be too difficult to seduce.

With no idea of the thoughts going through her partner's mind, Charlotte was protesting, "Oh, there is no way I could have a gown like that. I should not dare to wear it. It is too shocking!"

"Not even if *I* asked you to wear it—just for me?" His voice in her ear was soft, promising delights she could not know.

"I . . . I must think about it." But both of them knew that she would do as he wished. If it would please Graham, why should she not do it, Charlotte asked herself, while the young man smirked at the knowledge of his power over her.

Sylvia would never permit her to purchase such a gown as that, Charlotte knew, but Sylvia no longer accompanied her on shopping trips when other young ladies were with her. She had felt that Charlotte would appreciate having at least that bit of freedom from her supervision.

Charlotte felt a moment's trepidation as she approached Madame Celeste's domain; the woman was completely autocratic in her decisions about what one should wear. Then she reminded herself that, after all, Madame was employed by *her* and should be grateful for any trade she received.

The couturiere listened to Charlotte's description of the gown she wished, then exploded in Gallic fury. "Never!" she exclaimed. "Never would I so demean myself to make a gown of that sort—and especially for a *jeune fille*. That is the gown for a *demi-mondaine*—a strumpet."

"But . . . Madame . . . I saw one just like it at a ball last evening, only it was made up in red rather than white. Lady Caroline Lamb—"

"That is what I said."

"Well, if you will not make it for me, I am certain there are any number of other dressmakers in London who will do so!" Charlotte said angrily. Since Graham Floyd wanted her to wear it, the couturière's objection made her the more determined to have the gown.

"Oh, Charlotte, do you think you should do so, if Madame says it is wrong?" protested Rhoda Grey, her companion for today's adventure. "Remember, everyone in the *ton* abides by Madame's decisions."

"*I* do not intend to do so," Charlotte retorted, "if she will not permit me to have the gown I wish. After all, she is supposed to do as I wish about my clothing. As I told her, there are many other dressmakers in London. I am certain to find one who will do as I ask, even if *she* will not. However, you need not come with me if you are afraid of what people will say."

Rhoda, however, was completely under the other young lady's thumb and, overwhelmed by the scorn in the other's tone, meekly followed her from one shop to the next. None of the couturières on Bond Street would agree to the gown she wished, most of them echoing Madame Celeste's opinion, although not expressing it so forcibly.

At length, Charlotte found a small shop whose manager agreed to make the gown. After all, the Harmin crest on the carriage was recognizable, and the woman exulted in the thought that someone of such stature would appear in public in one of her gowns.

"Yes, I know the gown you mean," she said. "The lady has caused much talk by wearing it. I do not know whether it will be as striking if it is made in white. But I have a French silk which I think will do."

"And if it is trimmed in diamonds, rather than in paste gems . . . would that not be of help?"

"Oh, indeed it would, my lady. But the cost would be quite dear."

"That does not matter," Charlotte said recklessly. "Have it done as quickly as possible. I wish to wear it to Lady Ashburn's ball."

# CHAPTER
## ❧ 10 ❧

Before he spoke to Charlotte about the matter of her friendship with Graham Floyd, Bennett decided it might be best if he were to learn more about the gentleman. He wished to discover if the rumors Sylvia had heard were true or merely the sort of jealous talk that might occur when a young man became too popular with the ladies.

His own objection to Mr. Floyd was merely a matter of the fellow's personality; he considered the other's manners a bit too flamboyant for good taste, but that alone was scarcely enough to condemn him, since he saw many of whom he could say the same.

Bennett realized that he had paid little attention to the innuendos of the *ton*. So often they had no basis in fact but were merely the tongue-clackings of those who had little else to occupy their time. There were many who thought it amusing to destroy the reputations of others. He thought it wiser to ignore such tales.

In the case of Mr. Floyd, he learned that he should not have done so.

To atone for this earlier lack of interest, Bennett began applying to several gentlemen of his own age for more information about Graham Floyd. It took only a few questions to assure him that however bad the rumors might be, they were well-founded. The young man was part of a group of men of various ages whose libertine tendencies and love of extravagant and not too ethical gaming made them unwelcome in the homes of many of the leading families.

There was even talk that the group had founded a sort of Hell-fire Club. The truth of that particular rumor could not be proven, for members of so scandalous a group would not speak of their connection with it. Bennett encountered it so many times in his questioning, however, that he felt it must have some basis in fact. It was only because young Floyd was related to so prominent a family, he was informed by several friends, that he was not refused acceptance by the hostesses at all affairs.

"It seems that Syl—Lady Harmin has good reason to worry," he observed to a friend.

"If you mean about her stepdaughter's friendship with the fellow, she has reason indeed. If a daughter of mine looked in his direction, I should remove her from London at once."

Others spoke in the same vein. Even if no more than a part of what he learned about the young man was true, Bennett agreed that this was certainly not the sort of companion he wished for his friend's daughter. And if these were the rumors that had reached the countess, he

could understand why she was so anxious to remove
Charlotte from the fellow's influence.

It would be best, Bennett decided, if he spoke to the
girl when no one else was about, something difficult to
arrange since she was surrounded by her friends much
of the time.

He sent word asking if Charlotte would consent to
ride with him. Always pleased by the attention of her
longtime friend, Charlotte accepted at once. "But only
if you bring your curricle," she ordered.

"A curricle is not the best vehicle to use when taking
a young lady about," he protested.

"Oh, perhaps you are right, but I prefer it. It is so
dashing."

He shook his head over her choice of words, wondering if this was a sign she was already under the fellow's
influence, but agreed to do as she asked. When Bennett
helped her to the curricle's seat, then dismissed his tiger,
she slanted an amused glance at him. "Do you not think
that people will talk if they see us *a deux*?" Her tone was
arch, hardly the thing he expected from her.

"I doubt it," he told her with a laugh, wondering at
this bit of sophistication from her. "They will only think
you are accompanied by an elderly uncle."

"As if anyone could think *you* elderly." She slipped a
hand comfortably beneath his arm as he swung his horses
away from the house. "Are we not going to drive in the
Park?" she asked in disappointment when she saw the
direction he was taking.

"No, I wish to talk to you, not to half of London, as
we must do if we went into the Park at this hour. As you
must know."

"Oh, I do. All the world and his wife goes to the
Park each afternoon in order to be seen. That is why

I wished we might go there. I believed this was to be
an outing for pleasure, so I thought I could show you
off to my friends. None of them would be able to boast
of so distinguished an escort."

He smiled at this evidence of her naivete, hopeful that
this meant she was still untouched by Floyd's impurity.
Then, with an effort at sternness, he said, "Charlotte, it
would help if you were to be quiet for a moment, so that
I might say a word or two." He had guided the pair of
greys onto a less-traveled way, and could now give his
attention to her.

Charlotte pouted for an instant, unaccustomed to having any sort of rein on her pleasures. But her satisfaction
in being taken for a drive by Bennett was enough to
make her forget her pique. "Certainly," she said, folding
her hands in her lap and speaking with a meekness which
did not deceive him for a moment. "I am quite ready to
listen to anything you wish to tell me."

"You know, my dear, that I have always been quite
fond of you."

Her eyes widened. Was Bennett about to confess that
now that she was grown, he had developed a *tendre* for
her? Of course, she would not seriously consider the suit
of someone so old—why, he must be at least thirty—but
the thought of such an interest on his part was a heady
one. She nodded, waiting for him to say more.

"And the last thing I should wish would be to make
you unhappy in any way."

Better and better! She could scarcely wait for him to
declare himself. An offer—and during her first Season.
What a triumph that would be! She could see why he
should choose such an unorthodox spot in which to
speak to her. He would not wish Sylvia to know until
matters were settled between the two of them.

Naturally, she would accept him—after a moment of maidenly hesitation. Her earlier thought that he was too old had completely left her mind in the thrill of being sought by so fine a gentleman. Still, a betrothal did not necessarily mean that she would truly marry him.

And after word was spread among her friends that no less a personage than *Bennett Griffith* had shown her such an interest, doubtless many young gentlemen would follow suit. Perhaps even that interesting young Mr. Floyd . . .

"But there is a certain young gentleman who has been showing you a great deal of attention—"

"Are you saying you are jealous?" She could not keep still longer.

"Jealous?" Bennett could not control his amusement at the thought of his having any interest in this child except, perhaps, that of an old friend. The laugh that accompanied the word, however, was like a pitcherful of cold water thrown over her.

"Then what—"

"I merely wish to warn you that he is not a suitable companion. I am certain you know I am referring to Graham Floyd."

Charlotte glared at him. There could only be one person responsible for his saying that to *her*. "I knew it! It is my hateful stepmother who has persuaded you to say this, is it not? There is not a word of truth in the tales about him, you know."

"It happens, my girl, that there is a great deal of truth to what I am telling you. I have made enquiries about the fellow, and he is not a nice person for you to know. In fact, I learned that he is a good deal worse than many people suspect. If you would use your good sense for a moment—for I know you can be sensible when you wish to be—you would understand that I am only speaking for your good."

"Much you care about my good! And I do not believe you have made enquiries at all. It is merely that Sylvia has been telling you her usual sort of lies about him, and you believe her."

"You know that is not the truth."

"It is! And you should know by this time that she wishes to do away with all my friends. She has often told me that she will never agree to my marriage, so that she can keep control over my money." He need not know that Sylvia had said that only one time, when Charlotte had said she would marry as soon as possible to get away from her. Even on that occasion, Sylvia had merely said she would have to approve Charlotte's choice—but Bennett need not know that, either.

"I think you may have misunderstood her, and that she merely seeks the best for you. If it was proven that she deliberately tried to keep your fortune for herself, I would be the first—"

"No, you would not! I have been watching to see how she has bewitched you. Take me home at once!"

"Not until you promise me to give some thought to what I have told you."

"Not as long as you continue to go hand in glove with my stepmother."

"Now, Charlotte, if you would only listen—"

"Bennett Griffith, if you do not turn this carriage about and return me to Berkeley Square this instant, I shall get down and walk back home."

The threat stung him to anger. Did the little idiot not realize what could happen to a young girl walking alone upon the roadway—or anywhere upon the streets of London, for that matter? He caught her arm in a firm grasp. "You will do nothing of the kind."

Charlotte struggled against the hand which was holding her at his side, and Bennett realized that he could not keep her here except by force. And what if someone should pass and see him attempting to overcome a young lady? In her present mood, Charlotte might well claim that he was abducting her. "Sit still. I shall take you home."

She did not subside until she was certain that he was truly guiding his cattle back in the direction of the city. "Just the same," she told him loftily, "I shall never forgive you for listening to *that woman* and trying to ruin my life, as she wishes to do."

"No, it is you who wish to ruin your life, and you will do exactly that if you continue to be seen in the company of that loose fish."

Charlotte thrust her nose in the air and bit her lips to keep back the angry words, fearful of bursting into tears if she said anything more. What a triumph it would be for him and for Sylvia if they could reduce her to such a state. She could not remember when she had last wept for any reason. It had seldom been necessary to resort to tears to influence her father—and at all other times, a display of temper served her better than tears would have done.

Before the house, Bennett tossed the lines to his waiting tiger and moved to help Charlotte down, but she avoided his hand, leaping to the ground and dashing indoors. He followed her slowly, to find Sylvia anxiously awaiting him, while her stepdaughter pelted up the stairs to her room, slamming the door behind her.

He shook his head to the question in Sylvia's eyes. "I fear I have made matters worse, rather than better," he owned. "Charlotte thinks that I have moved into your camp and wish to keep her penned up so that you can keep her fortune for yourself."

"How ridiculous! If I that wished that, we should have remained in the country—at least, we might have done so until the earl ordered us away. Even then, I could have found some way to keep her confined."

"I think that might create something of a problem," he said ruefully.

"It would have done so, but I could have managed it, if that had been my wish. Certainly, I should not have planned this Season for her benefit. She should realize that. But I often feel that where I am concerned, Charlotte does not think. She has resented me since the day Martin brought me home—and I doubt there is anything that will make her change."

"I doubt it is so bad as all that." Even after he had witnessed Charlotte's display of anger against Sylvia, he felt that she was being quite as unreasonable in her way as was her stepdaughter. It was a fool's errand to attempt to come between two females, and he wished he had not tried to do anything of the kind.

Still, he had promised to do what he could to help her. Now he said, "However, if it will please you, I shall see if it is possible to warn young Floyd away from Charlotte. It may be a more difficult task now, as she is determined not to do as I asked."

"It is so kind of you to help." Impulsively, she put out her hand. When he clasped it, Sylvia seemed to feel a tingle running from his fingertips to the very core of her being. It was a feeling strange to her—a bit frightening, yet very welcome. She wondered if he might feel it, too.

Bennett held her hand, almost overcome by an impulse to draw her into his arms. She would have come to him willingly, he felt, remembering the day he had held her while they had laughed together over her unexpected callers, then wondered how he could have such feelings for her. True, Sylvia was a most attractive lady, but aside from concern for Charlotte, were they not opposed on every point?

In order to hide these strange emotions, he released her hand, saying more brusquely than he had intended, "It is the least I can do . . . for Charlotte."

"Yes . . . for Charlotte," Sylvia agreed and watched him go swiftly down the steps and leap into his curricle, whipping his pair to a gallop. For some reason she could not explain, she felt as if she might burst into tears. If only he could give as much attention to her as he did to her stepdaughter.

Having been informed that a parcel had come for Lady Charlotte from a shop whose name was unknown to anyone in the household, Sylvia went up to her stepdaughter's room, pausing in the open doorway to gape at the concoction Charlotte was taking from the wrappings.

"What on earth is that?" she managed to ask.

Charlotte whirled to face her. She had not intended to permit her stepmother to see her new gown at once, for she knew Sylvia would disapprove of it quite forcibly. It had been in her mind that she might be able to wear it, hidden beneath her cloak, so that her stepmother would not know of it until it was displayed at the ball.

Since Sylvia must see it sooner or later, however, this was as good a time as any. Charlotte held the gown before her, her chin upthrust defiantly. "It is my gown for Lady Ashburn's ball."

"Not that thing . . . you cannot be seen in it! I wonder that you could persuade Madame Celeste to make you anything so indecent." Then, seeing Charlotte's face, she said, "Of course—you did not purchase it from her. I was told that you had received a parcel from an unknown shop. This must be it. But of course, you cannot wear so disgraceful a gown as that."

"Why can I not? It is white, as a First Season gown must be—so there is no problem."

"Not if this were to be your First Season as a lightskirt hanging about the doorways at Covent Garden. No decent female would wear anything of the kind."

"You are wrong, for Caroline Lamb was wearing one just like this—only hers was scarlet."

"I think you know that the lady is not a proper model for you, or for any young lady, to follow. Her behavior has been scandalous, and if you try to copy her, you will soon find yourself ostracized by the *ton*."

"Nonetheless, I intend to wear this gown. Mr. Floyd thinks it is proper for me."

"Mr. Floyd," Sylvia said, attempting to keep her temper with the girl, "can scarcely be considered a good judge of what is proper. From the things I have heard about him, I should say he is quite improper, and not at all a good friend for you."

"I know you do not like him—and you have tried to prejudice Bennett against him as well. But I *do* like him and value his opinion. If he thinks this gown would be good for me, I shall wear it."

"You shall do nothing of the kind. The gown is going back to the shop today."

"You shall *not* send it back," Charlotte shouted, incensed by her stepmother's firmness, although her reaction to the gown was certainly not unexpected. "I refuse to permit you to humiliate me in that manner, treating me as if I were a child who could not choose her own gowns. Before you do that—" She snatched up a pair of shears, and before Sylvia could stop her, had slashed the gown in several places. "You may refuse to permit me to wear it, but at least, you cannot return it."

Sylvia stared at her, strongly tempted to order her to pack and return to the country at once. The girl was clearly not adult enough in her thinking for the London Season. It was only her own promise to Martin that made her hesitate to take her stepdaughter away at once. She had told him she would see that Charlotte had a Season.

"That was a waste of good money," she said when she had calmed herself enough to speak. "But if you wish to throw your money about, I can only be sorry for your lack of good sense. I suppose that the diamonds can be salvaged, so it will not be a total loss. But to be certain that nothing of this sort happens again, I am sending word to all tradesmen that no purchase of yours will be honored unless it has my approval."

Charlotte stared at her for several moments, then cried, "Yes, you have always wanted to rule me, have you not? Well, I shall show you yet that you cannot do so. And this is my room. Please leave me alone."

"Very well, but I suggest that you spend some time thinking of what I have said. For I intend to keep a tighter rein on you from this time."

She turned and left the bedroom, while Charlotte stared after her, too angry to speak.

# CHAPTER

## ❧ 11 ❧

It would be a simpler matter, Bennett thought, for him to speak to the foppish young man about his association with Charlotte than it had been to talk to the girl. Despite the rumors he had heard about Floyd's reckless behavior, he doubted the fellow was the sort who would stand up to the criticism of an older man.

Yet, when he attempted to raise the subject of Charlotte and their friendship, Graham Floyd looked at him impudently. "What is it to you what we do?" he demanded. "Charlotte—"

"—*Lady* Charlotte."

"If you like." The young man shrugged. "Although titles mean so little, do they not? Even my stiff-rumped grandsire has one, for all the good it may do him. I am far more able to enjoy life than the old man, who must subsist on draughts and gruels."

"I do not know your grandfather, nor is it my intention to discuss his way of life with you."

"I can see why you would not be interested in him— no one is, if they tell the truth about their feelings. He has never been worth a moment's concern, except to my uncle, who is anxious for him to die as soon as may be so that *he* may have the silly title."

"That has nothing—"

"Anyhow, referring to Lady Charlotte, as you were doing, she is a pretty little creature and I take pleasure in her company. It seems that she also enjoys mine." He brushed one side of his well-cropped mustache with a forefinger, then the other, as he continued. "Since that is the case, I can see no reason for you to interfere. I do not believe that you are her guardian."

Bennett kept a rein on his temper with difficulty. He knew now that his earlier impression of Graham Floyd as a mere fop was in error. His questioning of those who knew about him had revealed the young man's true character, that of a person of loose morals.

"No, I am not her guardian, but I am speaking because I was a friend of her father." It was his own father who had been a close friend of Lord Harmin, but he saw no reason to explain that. He had liked Harmin, too, and the details of the relationship were of far less importance than was Charlotte herself. "Therefore, I am naturally concerned with her ladyship's welfare."

"I think that Char—Lady Charlotte—if you are going to insist, as I can see you are—is quite capable of choosing her own companions."

"I doubt the young lady knows much about your . . . habits. The ones that have already caused you to be banned from many of the *ton*'s affairs. I may not be able to boast of any titled relatives—"

"As you see, I do not boast of mine."

"That is right. And I doubt they find anything about you of which they can boast. But what I was about to say is, even without a title, I do have some influence in the *ton*. A word from me in the right ears and you would find yourself cut off from the few places where you are still accepted."

Mr. Floyd looked at him, eyes narrowed. Was this old man—he must be thirty, at least—truly powerful enough to do as he threatened? The younger man knew that his own position in Society was perilous enough, and if word of some of his indiscretions should reach the ears of his high-nosed parent, which would be certain to happen if the *ton* rejected him, his more than generous allowance would be discontinued and he would be whisked back to the country at once, where his conduct could be more closely supervised.

It would mean the end of those deliciously scandalous escapades he and a few friends so enjoyed. When he weighed the pleasure of the lady's company and the opportunity of defying this gentleman against these other adventures, he was left with little choice.

"It may not be easy for me to do as you say," he conceded slowly. "After all, you can scarcely expect me to give the lady the cut direct."

"Certainly not. It would be most uncivil to treat her in that way, and I can assure you I should not like that any more than I like your present attentions to her. But if you no longer invite her to dance with you or ride with you, if you begin to make excuses at any time she should suggest a meeting . . . The young lady is intelligent, and it should not take long for her to gather that your interest now lies elsewhere."

"And if I do as you wish?"

"Then, of course, it will not be necessary for me to say anything. Your morals—or lack of them—do not interest me in any other way."

As Graham Floyd nodded reluctantly and moved away from him, Bennett congratulated himself on having won his point. Sylvia should be pleased, he thought. He then told himself sternly that he was not doing this to please the lady, but rather to protect Charlotte.

That was his only reason, was it not?

He shook his head, attempting to shut out the sight of the lovely Lady Harmin, who was smiling at him across the room as if she was certain he had done as she wished. Did she truly think she could influence him in any way, he asked himself, even as he made his way to her side to request the next dance.

She willingly placed her hand upon his arm and allowed him to lead her to the floor. Admiring the deep gold of her gown and the blue ribands trimming it, he compared her in his mind to a lovely gift, brightly wrapped and ready to fall into someone's eager hand. Might it, perhaps, be his hand that could grasp it? Was that what he wished? He shook his head to dispel the illusion, causing several of the dancers to look at him curiously.

As this was a country dance, there was little time for them to talk during the figures, but as the pattern of the dance brought them together, Sylvia asked quickly, "And will Mr. Floyd—"

At their next meeting, he was able to say, "I think you need have no worry." Then she was gone again. This was no way to carry on a conversation, Bennett decided, and said no more until he was leading her back to her chair after the dance was ended. Then he said, "It may take a little time to accomplish our task, but the young man has been persuaded to see the light and his agreed that he will do his utmost to discourage Charlotte."

Sylvia sighed deeply. "That is wonderful. I knew you would be able to hint him away from her. Now if she would only interest herself in some more worthy young gentleman, such as your friend—"

"I fear there is no chance for that. She seems to have taken him in dislike. It is a pity, for I know that Colin is deeply interested in her. But we can scarcely rule the tastes of another, can we?"

"No, as you say, it is a pity, for he seems to be a fine young man in every way. Except for his wish to enter the army, of course."

"It seems that the army must struggle along without his presence. I have not heard a word from him on that score since the evening I introduced him to Charlotte," he told her with a laugh. "If only her indifference does not cause him to change his mind again."

What was it about his laugh, Sylvia wondered, that made her feel warm and protected? How different he was from anyone she knew! Fearing that she might show her feelings too clearly, she said quickly, "I believe that Charlotte is still too young and too volatile to form a lasting affection for anyone, of course, but it would be a great relief to me if she were to choose friends whose interests marched with hers."

Bennett felt that there was much more he wanted to say to the lady—and, none of it to do with her stepdaughter. But he saw another gentleman approaching to claim her for the next dance, so he bowed and walked away. Perhaps it was a good thing that he had not permitted himself to linger; when he was near Lady

Harmin, his tongue seemed compelled to say things he knew he would regret later.

He must remind himself that she was the widow of his father's friend, and possibly—although he was no longer so certain of this as he had been when first he saw her— one who had married for the earl's fortune. If this was true, she was decidedly not the sort of lady for whom he should develop a lasting interest. Then why did it seem so important to him that she should be happy?

Sylvia accepted the partnership of the newcomer, but as he led her to the dance floor, she glanced back to the spot where Bennett still stood, gazing in her direction. For a moment, she thought, he had looked as if he had wished to say something more to her.

But what else was there to be said? He had routed the scoundrel whose attentions to Charlotte Sylvia had found so disturbing, and had accepted her thanks for his help in his usual fashion, making it clear that he had done as she had requested only out of consideration for Charlotte. Just as his offer to permit them to stay upon his estate had been made for the girl's sake, not for hers.

Well, that was what she had wanted from him, was it not? The gentleman could have no other interest for her. She no longer wished to bring him to her feet; yet, there were times when an errant thought smote her— indeed, she would prefer to have him in her arms. She remembered how wonderful his embrace had felt, then pushed that thought aside quickly. There was no way that she could be seriously interested in Bennett Griffith.

An exclamation from her partner made her realize that she had trod upon his toes, and she apologized, quickly resolving that she would put all thoughts of that other disturbing gentleman from her mind. He had

been occupying far too many of those thoughts these
past days—and sometimes even invading her dreams in
a most confusing manner.

As the days went by, Charlotte could scarcely fail
to become aware of a change in Mr. Floyd's demeanor
toward her. At Lady Smitson's ball, he had not once
asked her to dance. When she spoke to him, he had
merely bowed and passed by her to lead out another
young lady.

It might be that she had disappointed him by not
appearing in the daring gown he had suggested she
should wear—but would he not have commented upon
the fact, if that were all? She thought it more than mere
disappointment in her lack of bravery.

"So Sylvia has spoken to him," she said beneath
her breath. "I did not think even she would stoop to
such a trick as that. But there is no other explanation for the fact that he is now ignoring me. After
all, she was even able to twist Bennett, *my friend*,
about her thumb until he lectured me about Mr. Floyd,
saying he was not a suitable friend. He would never
have done so else. She is doing her best to ruin my
Season."

There must be some way that she could revenge herself upon her stepmother for her interference, something
that would make Sylvia quite as unhappy as she herself
now was. Charlotte could not fail to notice how often
Sylvia's glances went to wherever Bennett might happen
to be, glances she knew her stepmother was hardly aware
of taking.

So Sylvia had developed an interest in the gentleman!
What better way to be avenged than to take him away
from her, ruin any chances she might have with him?

She could do that with no trouble, Charlotte told herself, if she wished.

"After all," she reasoned, "I have known him so much longer than she. And he likes me, there is no doubt of that. He may have pretended that it was not merely jealousy when he spoke as he did about Graham Floyd, but I could tell that it was. Jealousy—and Sylvia's influence. That is it! I shall arrange it so that Bennett will make me an offer of marriage. Then we shall see what my stepmother has to say. She has been behaving as if this were her Season rather than mine. It is time someone made her pay—and I shall be the one to do so."

But what was the best way to go about bringing him back to her side? She had told Bennett she never wished to speak to him again, but certainly a little thing like that could be overcome. How many times had she said those same words to him when she was a child? He had paid no attention to them then; he would not do so now.

She had only to be a bit more pleasant to him than was customary and he would think she had overcome her anger. He might even think that she was seriously taking his advice to forget about Graham. Bennett was not one to hold a grudge, and he would not think that she would do so.

She smiled at him when he passed her and her partner for the next set, then said, "Bennett, you have not yet asked me for a dance. Are you angry with me?"

"No, I thought it was the other way about," he told her with a smile.

"With you? I could never be angry with you!" It was all she had time to say before her partner urged her to come away, but she knew that would be enough. Bennett would be at her side later.

Now she must concentrate all her attention upon this gentleman, unimportant as he might be, but who was asking jealously, "And who is he, that you should give him so much attention?"

"Who? Bennett?" Charlotte said airily. "I have known him forever. He was a friend of my father."

"Oh." Mr. Perkin was mollified. One must be kind to old friends of the family, he supposed. Such duty dances meant nothing at all, even when they interfered with a younger man's pursuit of the Beauty.

After all, the Beauty had agreed to have a second dance with *him*, later in the evening. Most of his friends must be satisfied with a single dance during the ball— and then only if she could find space for them on her busy schedule. Of course, he could not know she had been intending these dances for Graham Floyd, and had only granted them to this young man when the other had not approached her.

As Charlotte had planned, Bennett came to her side a bit later to ask, "Am I too late to claim a dance with you now, my dear?"

"Certainly not. It is never too late for your company," Charlotte told him with her brightest smile. To the younger gentlemen who were clustered about her, she said, "You must forgive me, sirs. This dance has long been promised to Mr. Griffith."

There were sighs and protests that she was being unkind to them, for the next dance was a waltz and most of them would have liked the privilege of holding the young lady and leading her about the floor. As Bennett whirled her away from them, he looked at the row of disappointed faces, then smiled down at her. "Little liar. You know I had not asked for any particular dance."

"Well, I had promised myself that I should dance with you, if you asked me to do so. So it was not entirely a lie, was it?"

"A truly feminine argument, my dear. But I shall accept it. I am only thankful that you have forgot your anger with me."

She looked up at him through her lashes, aware of the effect of such a glance. It had devastated any number of younger men, and she could not know that the smile it evoked from Bennett was one of amusement.

"Oh, that. I *was* angry for a few moments," she owned. "It seemed that you were attempting to interfere with my enjoyment of the Season. But I can understand now why you acted as you did—" He had done it to please Sylvia, but she would be avenged upon her step-mother for that, with no need to punish him further, especially when she depended upon his cooperation to secure her vengeance. "It is no longer of any importance."

"That is good. We have been friends much too long to come to blows merely because I wished to give you some good advice."

"Advice is not always a palatable thing, Bennett. You must know that. But as soon as I truly understood . . . I think you should know that I am not seeing the gentleman any longer."

She could not see any need to tell him that this change in their relationship was the gentleman's choice, not hers. Let Bennett think she had preferred to take his advice. It would please him and make it easier to carry out her scheme.

"I am happy to hear that." From her reply, he gathered she did not know that he had been responsible for warning the fellow away. As long as she did not, he did not mind that she took the credit for ending the growing attachment between them. To accept that Floyd had been the one who had made that choice would have been humiliating for her.

"And, Bennett—" Now was the time to begin pressing her advantage. "I am sorry that I ended our drive so quickly. Will you take me driving again, if I promise to say no more about what is past?"

"Gladly, my girl." How easily she was pleased, he told himself. Just like the child she still was. "And when would you like for me to call for you?"

"Tomorrow."

"So soon?" His eyebrows were raised. "Certainly you must have other engagements."

"Nothing that is of any importance—and I do have something I should like to speak about."

"Well, why not tell me now? I doubt that anyone can hear what we are saying."

"Oh, no. Not here. I . . . I should like some place more private."

"Very well." He spun her around as the dance ended. "Shall we say tomorrow at three?"

"That will be wonderful. But now, I suppose I should go and dance with some of the other gentlemen—but they are all so young."

"About your age."

"Yes, but a woman always feels much older."

Bennett bowed over her hand and restrained his smile until he was away from her. Little Charlotte, how amusing that she should think of herself as a woman. Why, she was still little more than a babe, with her thoughts flitting like quicksilver from one thing to another. See how quickly she had forgot her anger at him—and apparently had forgot young Floyd as well.

To his disappointment, he had no further opportunity to dance with Sylvia this evening, but at supper he paused beside her while her partner was busily filling their plates. "It seems that I am now once more in Charlotte's favor," he said softly.

"I am happy for that. You have been her friend for so long."

"Yes, she wishes to drive with me tomorrow. Doubtless she will deafen my ears with her rhapsodies about some new gentleman who now holds her interest, since she tells me she does not wish to see Floyd again." Her partner was returning, so he bowed and went on, happy that he was in the countess's favor as well.

# CHAPTER
## ❧ 12 ❧

Sylvia sighed as she looked at the large stack of papers that had accumulated upon her desk. Checking the accounts had never been her favorite occupation. Martin had always done so, however, and she tried to do as she believed he would have wished her now to do. While they were in the country, it had not been a difficult task, but to keep abreast of such affairs since they had come to London took a great deal of her time. There were so many new purchases, and always so much else needing her attention that she was inclined to be neglectful of these matters until Porton rather forcibly called her thoughts to the many envelopes he had placed there each day.

The household accounts gave her very little trouble. She knew how much more fortunate than most families she was in having a staff of honest servants, so there was never any sign of a tradesman's having overcharged her in return for a small "gift" to the cook or butler. If any had been tempted, Porton or Mrs. Hopgood would have caught the miscreants out and discharged them at once. These accounts were quickly marked for payment.

The personal accounts took more of her time. She was careful to check every item, indicating which purchases should be charged against her allowance and which should be paid from Charlotte's funds. There was some doubt about several small purchases, such as gloves or fans. She marked these to be charged to her. It made little difference who paid for these trifles, but she thought it better to pay for them herself rather than to begin a discussion with Charlotte about them.

There was one bill bearing an unfamiliar name, and Sylvia put it aside, intending to have Porton return it to the shop as having been sent to Charlotte in error. On second thought, she read it, gasping at the charge. Four hundred and fifty guineas for a ball gown, white French silk, trimmed with diamonds.

Of course, the monstrous creation Charlotte wanted to wear to a ball. The gown she said Mr. Floyd urged her to have made. She was certain at the time that Madame Celeste would never have touched so crude a thing as that. This Emmeline, or whatever her true name might be, must be doing well for herself if she had many clients as naive as Charlotte.

Since her stepdaughter, to avoid the "humiliation" of having the gown returned, had ruined it, there was no choice but to pay the account. Of course, it was all too probable that the woman would not have accepted its return, since there was little chance she could have found another buyer for it. Still, Sylvia sighed at the waste her stepdaughter's temper had cost.

She signed her name to the charge, marking that it was to be taken from Charlotte's account, but brightened at the thought that nothing of the kind could happen again. She had carried out her threat to inform the tradespeople that all such purchases must be approved by her.

Doubtless, Charlotte would consider *that* the greatest humiliation of all, but a great deal of money might be saved as a result of Sylvia's order. If the girl were permitted to throw away such great sums, she would soon have nothing left. Her share of Martin's fortune was not large enough to allow for such careless spending on Charlotte's part.

Several more small accounts took but a few moments to finish, and Sylvia pushed the completed stack to the back of the desk. On the morrow, Porton would have them delivered to Mr. Solicross for payment.

Charlotte had left her door ajar and had been peering through the opening. When her stepmother left her desk and descended to the drawing room, Charlotte slipped into the study. She had seen Emmeline's name upon the envelope as Porton carried the mail upstairs, and wished to see how much her reckless purchase had cost her.

"Four hundred and fifty guineas," she said furiously, but beneath her breath, so that no one would know she was here. In her determination to have the gown, she had not asked how much it would cost, though she remembered that the dressmaker had told her it would be "dear."

"Well, if Madame Celeste had made it for me, I do not doubt it would have cost twice as much. But it is a pity that I never had a chance to wear it. Of course, now that Mr. Floyd seems to have other interests, it would have been foolish for me to appear in it, since, being in white, it could not compare with Caroline Lamb's, after all. Still, it would have been worth the expense to have shocked Sylvia."

She looked at Sylvia's signature on the sheet and had a sudden thought. It might be that Bennett would be somewhat loath to agree to her plan; this might be useful in convincing him. She slipped the bill into her reticule and left the room as carefully as she had entered it.

That afternoon, Bennett again tooled his curricle to a halt before the Hamlin mansion. As he helped Charlotte into the seat, she cast a doubtful look at his tiger, and recalling that she had said she wished a private talk, he told the boy, "Wait here. We should return within the hour."

"Thank you," Charlotte said as they drove away. "I do not think I could talk freely in front of him."

"I am certain that Timothy is the soul of discretion," Bennett told her with a smile. "But it shall be as you wish. Shall we go through the Park today?"

She was not ready to show him off to her friends— yet. Time enough for that when she had achieved her aim. "No, please let us go where we were before, where there are not so many people about."

Obligingly, he took the less traveled way, saying, "And now, poppet, what is the news you wished to confide to me?"

"Not until we have reached a place where we can stop and you can give me your full attention."

A short time later, he halted the pair and said, "Will this be satisfactory?"

"Quite." Charlotte took a deep breath, then placed a hand upon his arm. "Bennett, will you marry me?"

Startled, Bennett allowed his hands to drop and the greys moved forward, accepting the gesture as permission to go on. He brought them under control once more, then asked in a half-strangled voice, "What did you say?"

"I said, 'Will you marry me?' "

"Charlotte," he forced himself to speak sternly, wondering if she was teasing him or if she was even aware of the implications in what she was saying, "this is not a matter for joking. You may make such a suggestion to the wrong man and find yourself on your way to Gretna Green before you know what is happening."

"Oh, we need not go there, but we can, if that is what you wish."

"Child, you cannot—"

"I am *not* a child!" She could scarcely stamp her foot while seated in the vehicle, but her tone held the same touch of fury. "I am quite old enough to know what I am doing."

"Nonetheless, *I* am old enough to be your father—at least, almost old enough."

"Only thirteen years. And when it is the man who is older, that is not so great a difference. I told you a woman always feels older."

"It is too great a difference for one of your age," he said more sternly than before. "And you must stop speaking in this way."

So he was not going to agree. Why should he refuse; she had thought it would be simple matter to convince him. If he had been as jealous of her attention to Graham Floyd as he had seemed, he should leap at the opportunity to accept her.

There must be something she could do or say to bring him around. The one feminine weapon she had never used, but one which should convince him that she meant what she said. "Oh, Bennett, you *must* help me," she cried, bursting into tears and flinging herself upon his chest. "I am so miserable."

When she threw herself across his arm, it caused him to jerk upon the lines and the horses danced a protest. Taking the ribbons in one hand, Bennett placed his arm about her. "My dear girl, nothing can be so bad as that."

This was better; he was being convinced, at least, that she was quite serious in her grief. She snuggled against him, wailing, "You do not know! Everyone thinks I am so happy in London, but I am not."

"Then why do you not tell me what is causing you so much grief?"

"It is Sylvia. She is determined to ruin my life. I have told you that before; I know you did not believe me, but it is true. If she can drive everyone away, keep me from finding a husband until I am of age, she will have four more years to do what she likes with all my money. That is why she hinted away Mr. Floyd."

"No, it was I who did that."

Charlotte's eyes blazed for an instant at the thought that he had also acted against her, but her face was still pressed against his chest, and she recalled her role before he could see her anger. "But it was Sylvia who asked you to do so, was it not?"

"True, but he was not the right sort for you. As I tried to tell you."

"Perhaps you are right." She toyed with his coat button as she spoke. "Graham Floyd might not have been the best of companions. It is so hard for a female to know these things without someone wiser to tell her what she ought to do. But it would be the same, no matter whom

I wished for company. Sylvia would try to drive them away. But she cannot object to you."

"I think your stepmother would have a great many reasons to object to your becoming my wife." Of course, Sylvia had once said she thought the pair of them would be well suited. But that was when they had first met— and he had said things which must have angered her. He thought her opinion of him was better now, had thought she even liked him. Could he be wrong about her?

"I can see how she has bewitched you," Charlotte accused. "But I can prove to you that she is cheating me. I took this bill off her desk today. See, she has charged this gown to my account. And you *know* I have never worn anything of that kind."

Overset as she might be, surely Charlotte would not say such things about Sylvia unless she had some reason for doing so. And he could read her signature quite plainly on the bill Charlotte held before him. He reached for it, but she refused to relinquish it.

"Every gown *I* have for this entire Season has been made by Madame Celeste." That much was true, since she had slashed the other rather than return it.

Seeing that Bennett was giving some thought to what she was saying, but fearing his feeling for her stepmother was still not destroyed, Charlotte increased her sobs until it seemed she was about to become hysterical. "You *must* help me, Bennett."

Her emotion seemed to affect the horses and they moved about uneasily. Bennett looped the lines about the edge of the seat and took out his kerchief to mop the tears from Charlotte's face.

"You must not weep in this fashion, my dear girl," he told her. "You will become ill if you continue. You know I shall help you."

She looked up at him hopefully; her weeping stopped as if his words were a magic spell. "You *will* marry me?"

"No, my dear, that would not do." Then as she showed signs of another bout of tears, he said hastily, "But I shall speak to your stepmother and tell her that I am looking after your interests. I believe I should have done as much from the first. Then there would have been no reason for you to be unhappy."

"Oh, if you would do that for me—"

"I have already persuaded Lady Harmin to bring you to my estate in Kent when the Season is over. I had not planned to spend time there while you are in residence, but I shall now pay a visit from time to time in order to see that everything is well with you."

"It is kind of you to offer us a place to live. And so is your plan of talking to Sylvia. You are so good to me, Bennett. But you know that your words would carry more weight with her if you told her we were to be married." What effect *that* would have on her stepmother! she thought, with inner glee.

Bennett, however, shook his head. Could the child not see how impossible such an arrangement would be? "No, I shall not do that. I am not the man for you, my dear. In fact, I had thought . . ."

He pushed the idea aside, but not before Charlotte had guessed what was in his mind. He had formed a *tendre* for Sylvia. It was quite unfair that he should do so, when Sylvia wanted to prevent *her* happiness. She began to sob once more, and Bennett was overcome by her seeming grief, just as she planned.

"But I shall make it plain to her," he continued, "that, from this moment, I shall be watching every penny she spends, to see that it is not your money. I am certain that if I go to your father's solicitor and tell him I am acting for you, he will give me the facts I need. And if Syl—the countess overspends her allowance again by as much as one farthing, I shall see that she is given in charge for attempting to defraud you."

Charlotte permitted her lips to quiver as if she were hiding her disappointment at his refusal to marry her, but she was well pleased with her gambit. In truth, she was happy that he had not agreed to her proposal. It would have taken her from beneath Sylvia's thumb, of course, but she had a feeling that Bennett's ideas of how his wife should behave would not please her at all.

She had been watching her stepmother closely and knew that Sylvia was beginning to place great value upon Bennett's good opinion. An opinion she was certain she had shattered for all time. And if Bennett *had* been thinking of offering for Sylvia, as she now suspected he might have done, she had put paid to *that* as well.

"Very well," she said in a low tone, wiping at tears that no longer existed, "if that is all you can do for me, I must accept your decision. I shall just have to continue to suffer my stepmother's cruelty."

"You speak as if she were in the habit of beating you and keeping you on bread and water." He had seen no evidence of any sort of cruelty on Sylvia's part, and was beginning to wonder how much credence he could put in what the girl had told him. How much of the tale of her mistreatment existed only in her imagination?

Charlotte was quick to realize that she might have said too much and knew she must rectify her error. "No, I must own that Sylvia has never *struck* me. She would not do that, I know, even if she were quite angry with me. Nor has she made any attempt to starve me. But,

Bennett, you know there are worse things than that. The way she discourages my friends, for example—"

"You must also own, Charlotte, that you have not always been wise in your choice of friends."

"Perhaps you are right about that, but she is not too concerned with whether they are right for me or not. *Anyone* I liked she would drive away."

"Very well. I think you are worrying too much about the matter, but I shall speak to her about that as well, if you wish. I shall make her understand that if I do not disapprove of your friends, there is no reason why she should do so. And I shall be watching her to see that she has no opportunity to drive them off."

She sat up, straightening her bonnet, and beamed at him. "Thank you, Bennett. I still think it would be best if you were to tell her that we were to be married, so that she would have no more power over me. But if, as you say, you will at least intercede for me so that I may have a *few* friends for the remainder of the Season, it will be of some help, I am certain."

"You may rest assured that I shall speak to her." He asked himself how he could have come to misjudge the lady. His first assessment of her had been correct, after all.

Charlotte placed her hand over his. "I am sorry to have subjected you to such a scene. I know that gentlemen dislike such things—or that is what I have heard. But I could turn to no one else."

He patted her hand before untying the lines. "You need never apologize for coming to me for help. I have always been your friend, and shall continue to be."

She gulped as if swallowing the last of her sobs. "Then I am happy that I spoke to you, even if I was such a watering pot."

She had not known how successful tears would be, but was happy that she had resorted to them. The effect had been *almost* what she wanted to achieve. Sylvia may have been responsible for spoiling her friendship with Graham Floyd, but at least, Sylvia's friendship with Bennett—if her stepmother's feeling for the gentleman did not go far deeper than that, as she suspected—was now ended for all time. Charlotte had made certain of that.

When they returned to Berkeley Square, Bennett tossed the lines to Timothy, saying curtly, "Walk them. I may be some time."

Timothy nodded, saying nothing. It was clear enough that the guv'nor was in a temper about something, and it was best to keep mum at such a time.

"I think it best if I go to my room at once," Charlotte said. She would have liked to overhear the scene she knew would come, but felt it wisest to absent herself, lest she betray her satisfaction.

"Yes, you are right." The poor girl had been so distraught that he did not wish to add to her unhappiness by forcing her to be present at his interview with Sylvia. He watched Charlotte go out of sight, then turned to Porton. "Will you inquire if Lady Harmin will see me?"

# CHAPTER
## ⇘ 13 ⇙

There had been a time when the butler would have refused the gentleman, but he sensed that there had been a change in her ladyship's feelings.

"If you will wait in the drawing room, sir," he said, "I shall notify her ladyship of your arrival."

Sylvia came down at once. Had he been able to persuade Charlotte that it had been the best thing to hint Mr. Floyd away from her? Had she perhaps mentioned that she had returned her interest to someone worthy, such as Mr. Waite? Sylvia was smiling as she entered the drawing room, but her smile vanished as she looked into his angry face.

"What is it?" she asked anxiously.

"I have just been speaking to Charlotte."

"I thought you would have done so, since you took her driving."

He stepped to the door and closed it firmly, much to

the disappointment of Porton, who was lingering in the hallway, and Charlotte, who had left her room to hang over the stair rail in an attempt to learn how successful her campaign had been. "Yes, she felt I was the only one to whom she could turn."

"You have always been her friend; I can see why she might confide in you. But you already know about her involvement with Graham Floyd. In fact, you were able to end it, for which I must thank you."

"And what of any other friends she might have? Have you been able to drive them away as well?"

"I do not understand. I have heard of no problems she has had with other friends. She has met a number of young ladies and gentlemen, all of whom are excellent company for her, I believe. As I told you, I could wish she would be a bit kinder to Mr. Waite, but she must make her own decision about that."

Her air of puzzlement—which, after his conversation with Charlotte, he knew must be feigned—appeared so genuine that it drove him to greater anger. "What is it that you do not understand?"

"Why you are so overset about Charlotte's friendships. There is nothing amiss there."

"I must tell you the child is so desperately unhappy that she asked me to marry her. She begged me to take her away from your influence."

Sylvia laughed hollowly. "I knew Charlotte disliked me—she has always done so—but I did not know her dislike would drive her to such extremes."

"Not dislike. Fear."

"Fear? Of me?" Sylvia laughed once more, then realized that the shrillness of her laughter might give the wrong impression. But what the gentleman was saying was so absurd she could not credit it. "What reason does

Charlotte have to fear me?" What tale is she spinning now, she wanted to add.

"That is what I asked, and she was almost hysterical in her reply. She believes that you will not approve of any marriage for her, so that you will be able to keep control of her money for another four years—to do with it as you please."

"And I suppose you were gulled by her story?" Sylvia's face had gone white; her fists were clenched. And she had begun to think the gentleman's opinion of her had improved. How wrong she had been! If he could believe such things of her . . .

"I told her I did not believe that you would do anything of the kind. I thought you had accepted a trust from your late husband to look after her welfare."

"As I did—as I have done."

"And what about buying expensive items for yourself and having them charged to her?"

"You think I would do that—that I would deliberately attempt to enrich myself at her expense?"

"I did not think so until Charlotte showed me the proof of her story."

"What?"

The shock in her tone halted him, but only for an moment. After all, he *had* seen the account. And Charlotte had told him that she wore no gowns other than those made by Madame Celeste. The other *must* be one of Sylvia's purchases; he did not know enough about ladies' fashions to judge whether her gown might have been purchased elsewhere. He decided that she was only shocked that he should have learned the truth about her actions.

"You are accusing me, Mr. Griffith, of nothing less than stealing from my stepdaughter. But of course, you would do so—I recall that from the time we met, you appeared to think that I was money-mad. You accused me at that time of having tricked Martin into a marriage so that I could get his fortune into my hands."

"Perhaps I was correct in thinking that," he told her recklessly. The lady's anger, which he considered to be unwarranted in the face of the evidence Charlotte had shown him, now made him forget how his feelings for her had changed in the past weeks.

Sylvia recoiled as if he had struck her. And she had begun to think more kindly of him—even more than that, if she owned the truth—and had thought he had come to do the same of her. Now he was willing to believe her stepdaughter's lies about her.

How mistaken she had been to trust him! To begin to care for him! Care for him? She knew that she loved him—a man who could think so badly of her. In his way, he was more insulting than Captain Lannon had been.

"I think it would be best for you to leave at once." The words almost choked her. "And you may be certain that I shall make some other arrangements for my stepdaughter and myself after the Season is ended. I would prefer that we should live in the dreariest attic rooms rather than to be indebted to you, even if that makes it more difficult to find a suitable match for Charlotte."

"Yes, I shall go, having no more wish for your company than you have for mine. But I warn you, my lady whether you come to my place in Kent or go elsewhere, I shall keep an eye upon you to see that you do not help yourself to any more of Charlotte's money."

He turned and strode out the door. Resisting an impulse—one which was quite foreign to her—to throw something at him, Sylvia followed him into the hall.

"Porton," she said so that Bennett could not fail to

hear her command, "Mr. Griffith is no longer to be admitted to the house under any conditions." And, catching a glimpse of the edge of Charlotte's skirt as the young lady drew quickly out of sight, she added, "He is no longer to be permitted to call upon Lady Charlotte, either."

The slamming of the outer door was Bennett's only answer.

Sylvia retreated to the drawing room, clenching her teeth upon her lower lip to keep from bursting into tears. They were tears of anger as well as of disappointment. Only now could she admit how much he had come to mean to her.

She recalled that Bennett had spoken of having proof of her attempts to cheat Charlotte. Since she had done nothing of the kind, there could be no such proof. What had Charlotte done to make him think that? She hurried upstairs to her study.

As Sylvia had instructed, Porton had taken away all the bills to be paid. All except one. Tucked beneath the corner of her blotter, as if in an effort to hide it— or perhaps to make it seem as if it had been lodged there by accident—was the account from the dressmaker Emmeline.

Snatching it up, Sylvia rang then waited impatiently until the butler hastened up the stairs. "When you took away the other accounts, Porton," she asked, "why did you not take this one as well?"

"Your pardon, milady, I did not take that because it was not upon your desk at the time."

"You are certain you did not overlook it? It had become almost hidden under the edge of the blotter."

"No, milady." The butler assumed his stiffest manner. "I did not overlook it. There was nothing upon the desk except the accounts I took at your order. In fact, I noted that your blotter was in need of replacement and ordered the maid to place a clean one there at once. Had there been a paper at that time, I could not have failed to see it."

"Yes, Porton, I understand." She knew at once that her suspicions about the account were correct.

"Shall I take it now, milady?"

"No, not now. I shall give it to you later. That will be all."

"Thank you, milady." Porton withdrew, content that her ladyship had accepted his statement. Either he or the maid must necessarily have seen the paper, had it been on the desk. Doubtless Lady Harmin had absentmindedly slipped it into a drawer and found it later. Unlike the employers of some of his friends, however, she was not so unfair as to blame a servant for her oversight.

The account in her hand, Sylvia went at once to her stepdaughter's bedchamber, rapping but not waiting for the girl's invitation before entering the room. Charlotte was seated at her dressing table, idly running a brush through her hair. Although she had expected Sylvia, she looked around in apparent surprise as her stepmother entered.

"You took this account from my desk!" Sylvia accused.

"Yes, after all, the account was meant for me. I wished to see how much the woman had dared to charge for the gown—the gown you would not permit me to wear." She knew now that without Graham Floyd's urging she would never have dared to appear in public wearing such a gown, but she would not give Sylvia the satisfaction of knowing that.

"Yes, the gown that could have been returned, had

you not destroyed it in a fit of temper. Well, you now know how much your pique has cost you. But you did not need to take it away merely to look at it. You took it to show to Ben—to Mr. Griffith, did you not?"

"Do you think Bennett would be interested in how much I spend upon my clothing?"

"He might be interested in your expenditures, if he had agreed to marry you, as he told me you asked him to do. But that was not the true reason you wished him to see this, was it?"

Charlotte's smile was mocking. "And for what other reason would I want him to see it?"

"To lie to him, to make him think that *I* had purchased it and charged it to you rather than to my allowance."

"I told him nothing of the sort. I merely reminded him that *I* had never worn anything in London that did not come from Madame Celeste."

Sylvia fought down the temptation to box Charlotte's ears. It would be useless, she knew; the girl had never been disciplined, and any attempt to do so now would only drive her to worse behavior. She was quite capable of telling Bennett and all the *ton* that she was the victim of her stepmother's abuse.

There still remained one threat Sylvia could use, although she disliked to do so. Still . . . "If you do anything of the kind again, we shall leave London at once. And you will be kept in the country until you have learned to behave." Charlotte could have no way of knowing that the earl wished to take possession of the manor and the Dower House, and they would have nowhere to go.

"You would not dare do that," Charlotte told her, but not quite as forcefully as she had spoken before. If Sylvia meant to do as she said—

"Would I not? Try me, my girl, and see what I should dare to do. And do not think you can appeal to Mr. Griffith. I am still your guardian!"

She turned and left the room, allowing the door to slam behind her.

For several moments, Charlotte paced the floor angrily. She did not believe that Sylvia would carry out her threat, but she would not wish to take the chance.

Then she began to smile, once more seating herself before her mirror and taking up her hairbrush. She knew that she had managed to put an end to Sylvia's budding romance with Bennett. Her stepmother was well served for attempting to win over *her* friend. She caressed her brush as she wondered what other mischief she might brew.

# CHAPTER
## ❧ 14 ❧

For the first time since she had come to London, Sylvia prepared for an evening affair with no sense of anticipation. She wondered if Charlotte realized how much harm she had done with her spiteful behavior. Harm, at least, to Sylvia's peace of mind.

"If she does know what she has done to me, how pleased she must be," she murmured. Hearing her voice, but not understanding the mumbled words, her dresser paused in her tasks, expecting to be given further orders. When her ladyship said nothing more, the woman shrugged and continued in her chore of clearing away her mistress's daytime wear and turning down her bed.

"You need not wait up for me," Sylvia told her. "We may be quite late."

The woman curtsied and withdrew, leaving Sylvia alone with her thoughts. She could not carry out her threat to take her stepdaughter away from London before the end of the Season, even had she been willing to do so. The new earl had taken possession of the manor house, and Sylvia did not doubt Miss Hodges was already busy converting the Dower House into what she considered a proper dwelling for her mother and aunt.

"No, we cannot go home, but neither now nor when the Season ends would I consider accepting Bennett's offer to allow us to stay at his estate in Kent." His accusations, although she knew that they had been fueled by Charlotte's lies, hurt too deeply for her to consider turning to him for assistance.

When they left Berkeley Square—which the earl, urged by Godiva, would expect them to do at the end of the Season—Sylvia would attempt to find a place for herself and Charlotte until the girl was ready to marry. Although as she now considered her stepdaughter ill-prepared for marriage, she knew that, when the time came, she would welcome the event as much as Charlotte.

"From what Bennett told me, she asked him to marry her," she said to herself as she gathered up her gloves and reticule and prepared to leave for the evening. "Since he wishes to protect her from me, why did he not agree to do so? It would have been so simple a solution."

Simple for everyone, she thought, except herself. But in such a case, she need not see either of them again. It would be a small consolation for her loss, but she reminded herself that, except in her wayward dreams, Bennett had never been hers to lose.

Charlotte, on the other hand, was looking forward to the evening with pleasure—except for one thing. As she allowed her maid, Polly, to help her into her new gown, she frowned at her reflection in the mirror. Charlotte was beginning to detest her white gowns.

The gown she had chosen for Lady Blakney's rout was becoming, as were all of Madame Celeste's creations, but she scowled as she thought of the outrageous gown Emmeline had made for her, and wondered if she would ever have dared to wear so daring a creation.

As they entered the carriage, she looked enviously at Sylvia's gown of sea-green net, worn over an undergown of silver satin. In her stepmother's place, she would have chosen claret rather than green, feeling the more vivid color more suitable. Any color except the white she was forced to wear. Had it been Sylvia who had ordered her to wear white, Charlotte would have defied her, but, except in the case of the scandalous gown, she did not quite dare to defy the maxims of Madame Celeste.

She told herself, however, that she should have insisted that her stepmother keep her mourning, even to bring her out. It had not occurred to the girl that Sylvia would be the center of a group of admiring gentlemen upon every occasion.

"A creature as old as *she* is," she said to herself, "should be content with sitting on the sidelines."

Charlotte noticed that there was one gentleman, however, who no longer joined the crowd about her stepmother. At the beginning of the Season, Captain Lannon had pursued Sylvia relentlessly, then apparently his ardor had cooled as quickly as it had arisen.

If *she* could manage to attract this gentleman, who apparently had ceased aspiring to be one of Sylvia's *cicisbei*, that would show her stepmother. Perhaps she could devise a way to draw away Sylvia's other admirers, one by one, until there was no one who would give her the least attention. As the young man to whom she had granted this dance swung her near the captain, Charlotte smiled broadly at him.

Startled by the young lady's obvious attention, Hugo nonetheless returned her smile and executed a half-bow in her direction, although green girls held little attraction for him.

An even easier conquest than she'd imagined! Charlotte told herself, and turned her attention back to her partner. When the dance had ended, however, she pointedly looked in Captain Lannon's direction once more.

The little minx was actually flirting with him! Hugo said to himself. And now he thought he recognized her. Was she not Lady Harmin's stepdaughter? If so, she might be worth cultivating . . . If only for her fortune.

The countess had decided to cut him for some reason he did not understand, but it appeared that the younger lady did not hold him in dislike. Being careful to choose a moment when Sylvia was otherwise engaged— for he feared her present animosity might extend to taking exception to his making the acquaintance of her stepdaughter—he approached Charlotte, reminded her that they had met before, and requested her company at supper.

"Yes, I should like that," Charlotte told him. Unlike the gentleman, she hoped that Sylvia would see the two of them together. Let Sylvia discover that *she* was succeeding where her stepmother had failed.

Sylvia saw the gentleman approach her stepdaughter and the girl accept his invitation. But she quickly recalled that she had once suggested to Hugo that he ought to ask Charlotte to dance, so she could scarcely object to his approaching her on this occasion.

He had reluctantly obeyed her request, she recalled, but she sensed no similar reluctance now. Of course, that earlier hesitance could have been feigned, because he was attempting at that time to impress *her* with his faithfulness.

She was not worried, however. She knew Hugo was in the market for a wealthy wife. Still, it was improbable that he would have approached Charlotte with such a thing in mind. Rather, he would prefer to marry a lady who was in charge of her own fortune, and he must know that Charlotte's money would still be in the hands of someone older, probably herself.

"Surely, he would know that," she mused, "and he must be aware that after I had dismissed him as I did, I should never approve if he made an offer for Charlotte."

Sylvia did not think Hugo Lannon was an evil man, although she had not forgiven him for his boast that he could win her and the fortune he thought was hers. Certainly, Hugo was not the only gentleman in the *ton* who wished to find a wife with money. That, she could have accepted. It was, rather, the manner in which he had bandied her name about before his friends that had angered her.

Meanwhile, she did not doubt that he would make an excellent dining partner for Charlotte. He was a clever conversationalist and knew how to make himself most agreeable. If Charlotte appeared in his company, it might serve to draw more eligible men to her side.

Her ladyship might have felt less assured if she had overheard Hugo saying, "I do not believe, Lady Charlotte, that your mother would—"

"Not my mother!" Charlotte said quickly.

"Your stepmother, then. I do not think she would approve of our being together."

"I am certain she would not." Charlotte gave him her most dazzling smile.

With an answering smile, he said, "And you do not mind if she disapproves?"

"No, it makes me happy to think that she does so."

Unaware of her attitude toward Sylvia, Hugo thought the young lady must have become so enamored of him that she would brave her stepmother's anger to be with him. If only he could play his cards right on this occasion, he might have his wealthy wife, after all.

During supper, he weighed his chances and before they left the room, he asked, "I know our acquaintance has been brief, so I hope I am not being too bold in asking . . . would you be willing to go for a drive with me tomorrow?"

Recalling his phaeton and the sleek pair of matched blacks, Charlotte said, "I should like that very much."

"Without your stepmother knowing that you plan to go with me, of course," he cautioned.

"I do not need her permission." She knew this to be untrue, but hoped he would believe her. He was certainly a man of the world; he must not be permitted to think of her as a child.

"Ah, but she might attempt to stop you from going . . . with *me*."

That was true enough, Charlotte said to herself; Sylvia would certainly do everything in her power to prevent her stepdaughter from meeting with a gentleman who was no longer interested in *her*. Would she go so far, however, as to take Charlotte back to the country, as she had threatened to do? Perhaps, but the girl doubted that Sylvia would risk having the *ton* think she was jealous of her stepdaughter. And the *on-dits* would fly swiftly if it was rumored Sylvia had taken the girl away because a former admirer now preferred the younger lady.

She tilted her head, pursed her lips as if thinking. She was aware of the enticing picture she made. "I *think* that could be arranged. Perhaps I can find I need a fitting on one of my new gowns. Sylvia does wish me to be well-dressed, although I cannot understand why she does so, since she clearly does not wish me to attract friends."

"But would she not accompany you?" It seemed to him that no lady ever missed an opportunity to visit her dressmaker. That must not happen. Although he did not suspect the reason for the lady's change in attitude toward him, he was certain that Lady Harmin would object to his friendship with her stepdaughter taking such a turn.

"Oh no, she does not always do so, now that all my gowns have been chosen." He need not know that Sylvia, having ordered the tradespeople to obtain her permission before filling any large order for her stepdaughter, no was longer worried about Charlotte's shopping trips.

"Not that I should have allowed her to choose them for me if I needed more. I shall merely take my maid, then have her wait for me while we drive. She will not dare to say anything to my stepmother. She knows I should dismiss her instantly if she did so."

So the girl was so brazen—or so naive—that she would be willing to ride with him unaccompanied. This suited his plan. "That is good. Then, where shall I meet you?"

Charlotte thought for a moment. "*Not* near Celeste's. I fear the woman is too much my stepmother's creature and would tell her in an instant. Shall we say near the Burlington Arcade?"

"And at what time?"

"Visits to one's dressmaker or such matters customarily take place in the morning. Would eleven of the clock be too early for you?"

"Certainly not," the captain said gallantly, and quite truthfully, considering the importance of winning over this chit. "I should be willing to wait all night for you if necessary."

He bowed and walked away, careful not to go near her again during the evening. He did not wish Lady Harmin to suspect that he was taking an interest in her stepdaughter; she would be certain to dash cold water on his plans.

Clad in a walking dress of rose-colored cambric with a matching bonnet—she thanked whatever powers that decided a young lady need not wear white when she was going about her ordinary tasks—Charlotte was waiting eagerly for the captain next morning when he drew his pair to a halt at the appointed place. With her was a meek young woman, who bobbed a curtsy and nodded when she was ordered to return to this spot in an hour to accompany her mistress home.

"I cannot remain away longer," the young lady explained as Hugo helped her to the phaeton's seat. "Else Sylvia might begin to wonder."

"I should be well pleased if we could spend the entire day together, many days, in fact. But I can understand your problem and shall have you back here in an hour. Now, where shall we drive?"

"I should like very much to have you drive me through the Park, so that we might be seen together."

He drew a deep breath, wishing to protest, when she continued, "But even at this hour, there is certain to be someone about who will carry tales to my stepmother.

I know . . . there is a drive toward the edge of the city where there are not many people about." It was the road she had taken twice with Bennett, and she exulted inwardly at taking another of her stepmother's acquaintances—even one who had grown cool toward her—this same way.

The drive was a pleasant one, and Captain Lannon was most careful to make his praises of the young lady's appearance flattering, but without seeming too forward on this first occasion. It was a simple thing to do, for Charlotte's beauty had won her a host of admirers, and she was accustomed to their adulation. Hugo was quick to recognize this, and as the drive progressed, he allowed his compliments to become a bit warmer.

# CHAPTER
## ❧ 15 ❧

It was the first of a number of surreptitious meetings. Hugo Lannon realized the need for haste in his wooing, and Charlotte soon developed a facility for making excuses for her absences from home.

She pled visits with a number of the young ladies she had met, sight-seeing with them, even paying visits to Hatchard's Book Store, although she had never before shown the least inclination toward bookishness. It was gratifying that Sylvia did not question her statement that Lady Ponsonby's nieces had encouraged her to read more books. Indeed, Sylvia was pleased that Charlotte was beginning to show an interest in improving her mind, although she sometimes suspected the girl would prefer the Gothic romances from the Minerva Press to more intellectual tomes.

Since Charlotte never entered the store, poor Polly

was forced to loiter about inside and to choose volumes that she thought her mistress might wish to peruse— a difficult task for the maid, who could barely read. Charlotte never read any of the books, but they were an unquestioned excuse. At other times, Polly was sent to purchase some trifle or other for her mistress as evidence of her outing.

Sylvia was happy that Charlotte had made friends among the other young ladies of the *ton*, and did not question her stepdaughter's frequent absences. She wished the girl would confide in her about some of the friends with whom she visited, but aside from the Misses Grey—at least, Sylvia supposed they were Charlotte's bookish friends; that family's lineage was quite complicated, so it was difficult to tell which of them was meant—Charlotte had never spoken of the others.

Sylvia knew it would be useless to ask Charlotte about her calls, for Charlotte would angrily accuse her stepmother of spying. This being the case, Sylvia suspected nothing.

Occasionally Hugo brought her gifts, small ones that he knew Charlotte could easily explain away. He was happy to see how little it took to impress the girl, so he did what he could to bring his suit to a swift conclusion.

It was necessary for him to do so; the Season would soon be over, and once the ladies had returned home, there would be no way for him to see Charlotte. Too, his many creditors were becoming almost insultingly insistent for payment. He knew they would not dare dun a gentleman in this fashion—but few of them classed soldiers as gentlemen, and their threats were growing stronger each day.

Charlotte had told Captain Lannon the same tale of

Sylvia's persecution as she had told to Bennett, and was led to believe that she was pouring her tissue of prevarications into a more sympathetic ear. Actually, Hugo cared little about her troubles at home, except as they might affect her attitude toward him.

Hoping he was not being too daring, he said, "But if you were married, you need not worry about what Lady Harmin might say or do. You would control your own fortune." Did the chit realize that the control of her money would pass into his hands the moment she became his wife? Apparently she did not, for she did not question his words.

Charlotte had said nothing to him of Sylvia's threat not to release her fortune if she married without her stepmother's consent. Once she was safely wed, she was certain she could depend upon her husband to help her fight for what was rightfully hers.

Looking up at Hugo through her lashes, she said with a demureness she was far from feeling, "I suppose you are right about that. But perhaps that is the reason she is careful not to allow me to meet any gentlemen."

"You have been meeting me, have you not?"

"Yes, but—"

"But you had not thought I would dare to speak so soon?" he said sadly. "Perhaps I am being too impetuous in doing so, but my dear Lady Charlotte, I should be the happiest man in the world if you would consent to become my wife."

The unexpected proposal startled Charlotte. She stared at him for several moments without speaking, for she had not thought beyond the possibility of winning his attention away from Sylvia. Certainly, marriage had not been a part of her plans.

This gentleman was not precisely the sort she would

have chosen, though he had been most gallant to her. And she was certain he would be easier for her to manage than Bennett would have been. Too, what a triumph it would be for her to have won a suitor away from her stepmother.

"I *have* been too rash." Hugo sounded contrite, "I have angered you."

"No, no," Charlotte said quickly. "It was a surprise, I own, but I am not angry." Should she tell him she had not dreamed he would offer marriage? No, that would make her sound too gauche. "Marriage is an important step," she went on, attempting to appear more mature, "one that requires a great deal of thought."

"Important? Very, but certainly you must have expected that I had more in mind than merely whiling away several hours in your company. It has been agonizing to be forced to watch you every evening meeting, dancing, with young men, men who are nearer your own age, while I did not dare approach you."

This much was true. What if the girl should fasten her attention upon one of them? His opportunity to attach her fortune would be lost.

Charlotte flushed with pleasure at his declaration. If it had made him so unhappy to see her with others, he must truly be smitten with her. This was her opportunity to rid herself of Sylvia's domination for all time. And with a gentleman who doted on her almost as much as her father had done. She was certain she could wrap him about her thumb just as easily as she had managed her father, and queen it over the *ton*—and especially over Sylvia.

"But how could we manage? Sylvia will be certain to try to stop me."

"I dislike to mention so sordid a solution to a delicate lady such as you. But the only way is an elopement."

"Elope?"

He heard the shock in her voice and said quickly, "I know . . . you are quite right. It is not done. But I can see no other way for us to be together. As you say, your stepmother will try to prevent you from marrying me in London. But when we return from Gretna, she will certainly be willing to permit a second ceremony, with all the pomp you deserve to have. A beautiful gown, a dozen bridesmaids if you wish, all the *ton* to wish us happy."

"Gretna?" Would she dare go there? Would she risk the censure of the *ton*? "I suppose we *could* prevent anyone except Sylvia from knowing that we had gone there. Afterward, I mean, we could pretend that the church service was the first one."

"Certainly, we could slip away as easily as we have been going for our rides. Once we were gone, with no one to know our direction, your stepmother would not dare to own the truth, but would give out word that you were ill. Then we could return to celebrate the elaborate marriage you wish. And you would be mine."

"I—" She was still a bit hesitant at the thought of an elopement. If word got out that she had taken such a step, she would be disgraced. She would no longer be accepted by the *ton*. Still, as Hugo had said, there was no other way to prevent Sylvia from stopping them. And once she was married, she would be her own mistress. Married women had so much more freedom; she had observed as much among her friends.

"Yes," she told him softly. "We can do that."

She allowed Hugo to embrace her, to kiss her, hardly aware of what he was doing. Her thoughts were busy with her own plans for the future, plans in which the gentleman figured only marginally.

"When?" he asked. "We must make it soon. I cannot wait to make you mine." A delay might mean that the chit would change her mind—or that his creditors might have him taken up for debt.

"As soon as we can do so." Why should they wait? She was eager to begin her new life.

"Why not tomorrow? Can you meet me exactly as we have been doing? Instead of our customary short drive, we can be on our way."

Charlotte pursed her lips, thinking. She could send Polly to Hugo's rooms this evening with a bag of her clothing. Then they could leave tomorrow. With no idea of the distance between London and Gretna Green, she told herself that before Sylvia knew that she was missing, she would be a married woman. She would be free of her stepmother's rule—completely free.

As always, Polly had done as she was told. But she could not convince herself that it was right for her mistress to go off in this way with a gentleman. It had been bad enough for the lady to meet him secretly; to plan a runaway marriage was much worse. Ladies did not do such things, even a serving girl would not consider such a step unless she were in trouble. Could Lady Charlotte . . . ?

Still, she had been ordered to keep silent about Lady Charlotte's plans. What should she do? When her ladyship had gone for secret rides with the gentleman, her place had been to wait for her mistress's return. She could not loiter about the streets for the entire day, but if she returned home without her mistress, it would be necessary for her to answer questions. And she knew she could not lie successfully.

She had therefore spent as much time as she dared in

some of the shops in the Arcade; then, because she could think of nothing else to do, reluctantly she returned to Berkeley Square. At the first sight of Lady Harmin, she burst into tears.

"What is it?" Sylvia asked her anxiously. "Has something happened to Lady Charlotte?"

"Oh, milady, milady," Polly said between sobs. "I do not know what I ought to do."

The girl was crying so hard, her sobs now punctuated with hiccups, that several minutes passed before Sylvia could quiet her enough that she could speak coherently. Then the entire story came tumbling out, Polly alternately blaming herself for not having spoken sooner about what was happening and excusing herself because she must obey her mistress. Once her first fears that Charlotte might have been injured in some way were proven groundless, Sylvia was quite angry at her stepdaughter for behaving in so foolish a manner.

Finally, Polly sobbed out her question about the possible reason for an elopement. Sylvia fiercely ordered her to be quiet; even this girl should know that Charlotte's foolishness would not have carried her to such an extreme. However, she was now frightened at what *might* happen to her stepdaughter.

Hugo Lannon would know that Sylvia would object to his marrying Charlotte. If he truly planned marriage, it would have to be done secretly. But was there any way that a secret marriage could be arranged? And how could she prevent it?

Even worse, what if Hugo did *not* intend to marry the girl, but only to ruin her? Hugo was doubtless quite angry with her for having cut him as she had done. Would his anger be great enough that he might think his best revenge would be in harming her stepdaughter?

Common sense told her, however, that since Hugo needed money so desperately, anything except marriage would be useless to him. His plan *must* be a marriage to Charlotte before her stepmother could object.

"Do be quiet, Polly," she ordered the girl, who had again begun sobbing. "No one can blame you for what has happened. You only did as you were told. I wish you had come to tell me sooner what was happening, but I can understand why you did not. When she wants her way, Lady Charlotte can be very determined. Now I must decide what to do. Did she say where she was going?"

"No, milady, not a word. Only that I was to take some of her clothing along to Captain Lannon's rooms last night. And that I must be sure not tell anyone that she was going away today. But how could I be quiet, when questions were sure to be asked?"

"No, you could not. And it is a good thing that you came to me when you did. Now, stop your crying. I shall take care of everything."

With no idea of how to begin searching for the missing girl, Sylvia ordered out her carriage. Bennett will know what to do, she told herself. He will blame me, of course, for not watching Charlotte more carefully, and he will be right.

Even in her haste to be after her stepdaughter, she took special pains in her dressing, choosing a walking dress of her favorite deep violet with a matching fur-trimmed pelisse. She felt that could not go to Bennett, to ask for his help, unless she looked her best. Still, no amount of attention to her appearance could banish the expression of deep concern from her eyes.

Edmonds concealed his surprise when she ordered him to take her quickly to Mr. Griffith's rooms. However, he did as he was told, helping her to alight, then holding the cattle when she ordered him to wait.

Like all the members of the household, he had heard something of Lady Charlotte's latest escapade, and wondered if this was the cause of Lady Harmin's unusual behavior. Was it possible that Polly's suspicions about her mistress were correct—that this was a marriage of necessity? Sylvia had ordered the girl to be silent when she had made such a suggestion, but rumors had flown about the household.

Bennett had just finished luncheon and was still at the table, twirling a glass between his fingers as he talked with his guest. Despite her feeling of urgency, Sylvia halted at the sight of Colin Waite. She had not considered he would be present, and did not wish to broadcast the news of Charlotte's foolish behavior. However, Bennett came to her at once, taking both her hands in his comfortable grasp.

"You are in trouble?" he asked, quite as if they had not parted in anger. "How can I be of help?"

Sylvia wished she could throw herself upon his chest and beg his forgiveness for her part in the quarrel. But this was neither the time nor the place for such acts. Forcing herself to remain as calm as possible at this trying moment, she said, "Not I, but—"

She cast a doubtful look in the direction of Mr. Waite.

"If it concerns Charlotte," Bennett said, "and I assume it must if you are in no trouble, you need not mind if Colin hears what you have to say. Despite her treatment of him, he holds the girl in the highest regard."

"More than mere regard; I love her," the young gentleman said, as stubbornly as if he expected someone to dispute his words.

All the more reason he should not be told what Charlotte had done, Sylvia thought, but both gentlemen were waiting for her to speak. She could not remain silent, not if she was to help her stepdaughter. She could only hope that the young man would not be too greatly angered by the girl's recklessness.

"She has run away," she said at last.

"Run away? Have you quarreled?"

Recalling Bennett's accusations at their last meeting, Sylvia felt that he was blaming her even without knowing the entire story. She was tempted for an instant to turn away and seek aid elsewhere. But there was no one else with whom she could trust the tale.

"No, in fact, matters have been going quite smoothly between us these past days. So much so that I ought to have suspected something was amiss. Charlotte has not been careful of my opinions in the past."

"You may recall that she told me something of how matters stood between the pair of you."

"Whatever she told you was highly colored, I am certain. However, that does not matter now. Her tales have been that she has been shopping or visiting with other young ladies, and I was happy that she was doing so and did not wish to put too tight a rein upon her pleasures. I learned only today—from her maid—that instead, Charlotte has been secretly meeting with Captain Lannon."

"Lannon!" Colin leaped to his feet. "Why should she wish to meet with him?"

"Doubtless because he has flattered her highly. I can imagine only too well what he might say."

*Yes, you must have had good opportunity to learn about his gallantry before whatever occurred that changed your mind about him,* Bennett said to himself. However, this was no time to speak of such matters. He had been aware that since the day he had ordered the fellow out of her house, Sylvia had avoided him at all gatherings.

Knowing the girl, it was probable, he thought, that Charlotte had not become interested in Lannon because of her stepmother's attentions to him. Quite the opposite. She had taken him up because Sylvia had cast him off. "And you did not notice any sign of growing friendship between them?" he asked.

"Not at all, there *was* no sign. No outward sign, at least. I should have said that they were no more than barely acquainted. They shared a supper at Lady Blakeny's rout last week, but I have not seen them exchange a word at any of the affairs since that time. But I thought nothing of that; he is not the sort I should have suspected of having an interest in so young a girl. Of course, I ought to have remembered his need for money. Or I did so, but thought he would know she did not have control of her fortune."

Belatedly, Bennett offered her a chair and poured her a glass of wine. As Sylvia sipped it, he enquired, "Then how can you be certain of what she has done?"

"She has been going out for several days, to visit her friends, the dressmaker, various places. Polly tells me that all of these visits were mere fabrications, that Captain Lannon has been taking Charlotte up for drives, while the maid has been left to await her return."

Colin murmured something beneath his breath, but Sylvia was certain he had been swearing. She could scarcely blame him; this was doubly unpleasant news for him if he truly loved the girl.

"If the two of them had been seen driving about the countryside alone, Charlotte's reputation would have been in ruins. But that is nothing to what they have done now. Hugo has apparently managed to persuade her to run away with him. And I have not the faintest idea where I should begin to search for her."

Wishing he might take her in his arms and comfort her, Bennett forced himself to remain calm. This was clearly not the time to air his feelings for the lady. "It is unlikely that Charlotte would agree to an elopement of this sort unless she thought he meant marriage?"

"No, I too, am certain she would not go else, reckless as she is at times. She would not carry her dislike for me to such an extreme. Then, too, if it is probable that Hugo has his eye upon her fortune, he may think that once they are wed, it would fall into his hands. I have thought about it all the time I was on my way here, until my head is spinning, and I am certain they are planning marriage."

"Then they would be taking the Great North Road."

# CHAPTER
## ❧ 16 ❧

"T—toward Gretna Green, you mean?" Her hand trembled so that the wine almost spilled from her glass. Bennett removed it and set it upon the table.

"Why not?" He forced himself to sound calmer than he felt. "There is no place nearer where he could wed the girl. I believe I know Charlotte well enough to know that she would never consent to a Fleet marriage, and I doubt if Lannon would have gone to the expense or trouble of obtaining a special license. Since Charlotte is under-age, it would not be issued unless they had proof of your consent."

Colin again growled something beneath his breath, but Sylvia nodded. "You must be right." Her tone was unhappy but resigned.

Bennett caught her hands once more, squeezing them as if to offer what comfort he could by his touch. "You must not worry; we shall overtake them. I can have my carriage out in a trice."

"Mine is outside." She rose, still clinging to his hands, feeling they were the only steady force in her madly whirling world.

"Good—that will save time. Colin—"

"You will go nowhere without me," the young man said firmly.

"But . . . but . . ." Sylvia was certain that, should they catch up with the runaways, the last person Charlotte would wish to see—aside from herself—would be the gentleman who had paid her so much attention.

"Lady Harmin, you can refuse me a place in your carriage, I know. But if you do so, I shall order out one of Bennett's mounts and follow you. You cannot prevent me from going after the young lady I love."

Sylvia sighed and shook her head, feeling tears behind her eyelids. If Charlotte only knew what she had risked losing by her mad act . . . "In the face of such devotion, young sir, I can hardly refuse to permit you to accompany us. But let us go as quickly as we can."

Offering his arm, Bennett asked, "Do you know how long they have been gone?"

"According to what Polly said, they drove away about eleven o'clock."

"Then we should have no trouble in finding them. It would have taken them some time to get away from London, as there would have been a number of carriages on the streets at that hour, and they would not have wished to draw attention by traveling too quickly."

Bennett handed Sylvia into the carriage, then conferred with her driver for several moments before he entered and took his place beside her. Colin sat opposite them, clenching and unclenching his fists as he thought of

Charlotte being carried away from him. Why had she done this? he asked himself. What attraction could a man of Lannon's stamp hold for her? "Can we not go faster?" he demanded.

"Relax, lad," Bennett said reassuringly. "We are traveling at a good speed now. Better than our runaways, I am certain. As we get farther from the city, however, I have ordered the driver to go slower, so that we can look at the various inns we pass."

"You think, then, they will have stopped somewhere?" Sylvia asked.

"I am certain they will have done so. It is a journey of several days to the border. And since they will doubtless not think they are being pursued, they will feel no need to make undue haste. I have no doubt Charlotte will insist upon calling a halt by the time darkness has fallen."

"But that is worse . . . to stay at an inn—" Colin began, fidgeting as if he wished he might leap from the carriage and run ahead.

"What else can they do?" Bennett asked him reasonably. He could understand and sympathize with the young man's impatience, so he wished to reassure him. "But we shall find them soon after they stop. There is no need to worry."

His calm tone belied Bennett's own inner worry. He could only hope that he was right in his estimate of what the pair would do. What if Lannon had not planned to go to Gretna, but knew of a friendly vicar who might be persuaded to perform the ceremony, even without the necessary license? Such a marriage would hold, he knew.

For an instant, he felt like raging at Sylvia for not having foreseen that something of this kind might happen and for not keeping a closer watch over the girl. Then he forced himself to look at the situation sensibly.

There was no way that the lady could have known what Charlotte would do. No one could do *that*!

He recalled the afternoon Charlotte had begged him to marry her. At the time, he had thought her sincere in her statements about Sylvia's determination to keep her under control in order to pilfer her fortune. But afterward, although he had accused Sylvia of doing just that, he realized that Charlotte had doubtless been playing upon his long-time friendship.

There had been no proof that the account she showed him had been for one of Sylvia's purchases, merely because she had signed the bill for payment. He did not stop to consider why Charlotte might have pretended her stepmother was cheating her, but had only thought it was like the girl to act before she thought. Doubtless, that was what she was doing when she agreed to run away with Lannon.

Sylvia had told him that Charlotte disliked her; although he had thought she was exaggerating the girl's feelings toward her, he had seen no evidence that the lady had in any way been cruel to her stepdaughter, as Charlotte had claimed. On the contrary, Sylvia was doing what she could to bring the girl out in the proper fashion. True, she had objected strongly to Charlotte's growing interest in Graham Floyd, but his own investigation had shown that the young man was no fit companion for Charlotte.

He had known that Harmin had spoiled his daughter in many ways. And as a headstrong girl she was determined to have things her way. In her wish to free herself from the constraints, she would have been an easy prey for a smooth-talking fellow like Lannon.

They had passed the limits of the city, and he could feel the carriage slowing as they reached an inn, but he tapped on the roof to signal the driver to go on.

"They would not have halted this soon," he explained to Sylvia and Colin, both of whom were quite as worried as he but less able to hide their feelings.

Several times in the next hour, the carriage was halted at inns while Bennett checked for any sign of the runaways, only to return to his place with a sign to the driver to proceed.

"Surely they must have stopped by now," Sylvia's voice showed her tension. "It is already full dark, so unless they planned to drive through the night—"

"Hardly that, I am certain, since they are not fearing pursuit. I think Charlotte, at least, would demand her comfort."

Sylvia nodded, grateful for the hand holding hers in the darkness. She was so overset at the thought of Charlotte's elopement that she could never have made this journey without him at her side. If only she could be as calm about this as Bennett. But, for all his friendship with Charlotte, he could not have the feeling for the girl that she did.

Charlotte could be quite exasperating at times—lord knew she had been especially so since they had come to London—but Sylvia could never wish her harm.

Bennett had released her hand. Sylvia wanted to catch him back, until she realized that he had leaned from the carriage window to order the driver to halt.

"Here, sir?" the man asked incredulously, looking at the mean building at the roadside.

"They would not stop *here*," Colin protested, as certain as the driver that Charlotte would never have agreed to stay in so humble a place.

"They might have done. Doubtless, Lannon's pockets are none too well filled, so he would choose a place where the prices are more reasonable and the help less inclined to ask questions. And although I cannot be certain, having only seen it twice, I believe that carriage might be his."

"Then we had best make certain," Sylvia declared. She was about to follow Bennett from the carriage when he put out a hand to stop her.

"It might be better if I went alone."

"No, if Charlotte is here, I want her to know we are thinking of her."

He shook his head, knowing it was useless to protest, and stalked to the inn door, Sylvia and Colin on his heels. They had barely opened the door to the malodorous tap room when they could hear Charlotte angrily demanding to return to London.

"Oh no, my dear," Captain Lannon told her. "Not so soon as this."

"But I have decided that I do not wish to go to Gretna Green with you, after all. I did not know it was so far from London . . . that we would have to spend several days upon the road."

"Quite right, my girl. It is a great distance and we shall not there. We shall return to London as you wish. But we shall not do so yet."

"If you will not take me, I shall go alone." There was a sound of scuffling and Charlotte cried out, "Let me go, sir. I have told you—"

"—And I have told you we shall return to London— in the morning. After she learns that you have spent the night with me at an inn, your stepmother will be only too happy to give her consent to our marriage."

"No, I shall never consent to staying here, or anywhere, with you. And I do not wish to marry you, after all. Since you refuse to take me home as I ask, I shall speak to the landlord. Certainly, he will have some sort of conveyance I can use."

"Oh yes, I am certain that he has. However, I can assure you that he will not permit you to use it—nor go anywhere without me."

Colin would have rushed toward the sound of the voices, but Bennett shook his head and thrust out an arm, holding the younger man back, then led the way into the tiny room which served as a private parlor. Hearing the door open, Hugo thought it was the innkeeper who intruded and began, "I told you to stay out until I called—" He broke off, recognizing the trio who entered.

For an instant, Sylvia thought that Charlotte was about to run to them for protection. She had half-extended her arms to take her, then the girl drew herself together and demanded, with as much dignity as she could muster, "What are you doing here?"

"I think that should be quite obvious," Bennett told her, then ordered, "Colin, take Charlotte to the carriage. Go with them, Sylvia."

"Not with her. I prefer to remain here," Charlotte said stubbornly.

"It did not sound as if that was your wish when we came into the room." He nodded toward his young companion. "Do as I say!"

Sylvia motioned to the younger man to obey, but as he placed an arm about Charlotte's shoulders and attempted to draw her out of the room, the girl struggled again him. "No, I shall stay here. You cannot make me go!"

Colin shrugged but made no further effort to take her away, having no wish to hear her loud protests as he carried her from the room.

Sylvia wished that Colin had been able to remove her stepdaughter, but stood her own ground, determined not to leave Bennett's side.

"I told you to leave." Bennett was beginning to remove his coat as he spoke.

"No, I cannot allow you to fight him."

"Does he still mean as much as that to you?" There was bitterness in Bennett's tone.

"Oh, no, not Hugo." She moved a step closer, reached out to touch his left shoulder gently. She knew he declared that he had completely recovered, but she had seen that there were times when his wound still troubled him. "You would be hurt—or at least, you might be— if you fought him. And it is not necessary."

The anger left Bennett's eyes at this evidence of her concern for him rather than for the other man. "But, my dear, after what the man has done, you must know you cannot persuade me to let him go unpunished."

A warmth went through Sylvia at his words, the first endearment she had heard from him. And spoken at a time like this, the words must have been intended. "Certainly I should not wish that. But there is a better way." She turned to face Hugo, who had been watching the pair of them, a cynical smile upon his lips.

"So you intend to shelter him behind your skirts?" Hugo said with a sneer.

"Not at all, Captain Lannon. I may tell you that I should take the greatest pleasure in seeing Bennett give you the drubbing you fully deserve for attempting to run off with a young girl. However, before you come to blows, as both of you seem willing to do, I think you should know this. If you had succeeded in marrying Charlotte, she would not have had a penny."

"You need not try to make me believe that. All London

knows that the chit is an heiress."

"Certainly I am," Charlotte put in.

"Be quiet, if you are to stay here. Otherwise, go to the carriage," Sylvia bade her stepdaughter. To Hugo, she said, "But do they know that she has the money only if her marriage has my consent? And I should never consent to allow her to marry *you*."

Charlotte muttered something her stepmother could not hear. The three men ignored her, all now staring at Sylvia. Bennett was beginning to smile as he recalled that Sylvia had told him this some weeks ago; Colin looked as if he wished to cheer her words; and Hugo appeared to be completely astonished. "You mean that you would go so far as that to prevent my marrying someone other than yourself—and after you have treated me so coldly?" There was a note of self-satisfaction in his tone, a satisfaction that she destroyed at once.

"Not anyone else, Captain Lannon. You may marry whomever you like, for all that I care. But not Charlotte. I am responsible for her, and I would do whatever is necessary to prevent your marrying her." She was surprised that Charlotte said nothing further; it would have been quite like the girl to argue at this point.

"You have twice referred to this fellow as Captain Lannon," Bennett said.

Sylvia nodded. "Certainly. That is who he is. A member of the Duke of Wellington's staff. One would think such a man would be above abducting young girls."

"There was no—"

"Oh, his name is Lannon, certainly," Bennett interrupted the other man's protest. "But not a captain. The fellow is a common soldier. And I doubt if he has ever laid eyes upon the Duke; certainly, he is not a member of his staff."

The others stared at him. "But what makes you think that?" Sylvia asked.

Bennett shrugged. "Since that day the fellow attempted to browbeat you, I have had him investigated. What I am saying now is what I learned about him."

"But why did you not tell us sooner?"

"I should have done had he offered you any further trouble. Since he did not, I saw no reason to spoil his game. Of course, had I known he was pursuing Charlotte, I should have spoken at once."

"I do not believe it," Charlotte said angrily.

"I do," her stepmother stated. "Doubtless that is one reason he was so eager to find a wealthy wife—someone who might shield him when the truth of his masquerade became known."

"But, Sylvia . . . Lady Harmin . . ."

"Now I can see that I should have told you—what do I call you?—about my prospects. I did not tell you the reason for my decision when I told you you were no longer welcome in my house. Perhaps it was unfair of me not to have explained why you were being dismissed, but I told myself that you did not deserve an explanation of my change of opinion about you."

"It was unfair. I had done nothing to cause you to act as you did."

"That is not quite true, sir. You see, I happened to overhear several of your friends laughing together about your boast to them that you could so easily wind the widow about your thumb, that you would soon have her—and her money. Doubtless, they, too, knew that you were not what you appeared."

Behind her, she could hear Charlotte's gasp and Colin's angry growl.

It was Bennett, however, who spoke. "He said that—

about you?" Forgetting that there had been a time when he had accused her of angling for a wealthy husband, he started toward the other man again. But Sylvia placed a hand upon his chest, and shook her head. "No you must not."

"But . . . but, Lady Harmin, you must have known . . ." Hugo Lannon was speaking eagerly in an attempt to restore himself to her good graces, although he must have known such a thing was an impossibility in the face of his latest actions, as well as the revelation of his other deceit. "A man is sometimes indiscreet in speaking to friends. That was what had happened, I assure you. It did not mean I did not hold you in the deepest regard. You know that I should never have looked twice at the girl had you not dismissed me so cruelly."

"Oh yes, I can believe that. For if you thought you could have my fortune, you would have had no reason to wish for Charlotte's."

Charlotte gasped again and began to speak, but Colin quieted her as Sylvia continued. "But I must tell you now what I was too proud and too angry to say then. You see, the rumor-mongers of London do not always know the truth. *My* allowance from my late husband stops the moment I marry someone else."

"You only say that now," Hugo said angrily, "to excuse the way you first encouraged me, then decided to throw me over because I injured your pride."

Sylvia could feel Bennett stir, but pressed his shoulder to persuade him not to take action on her account. "You must believe me. I never intended to encourage you, Hugo, although you may have thought I was doing so."

"Certainly, I thought that. So did everyone who saw us together."

"If that is so, I am sorry for it." Both men could hear the sincerity in her tone. "Even now that I know the truth about you. But tell me honestly, if I had told you that I should lose my allowance when I married—not that I ever should have about my prospects, for I did not feel that we were close enough to take you into my confidence about such matters—and if you had known that, would you have continued your . . . shall we call it 'pursuit' of me?"

The self-styled captain stared at Sylvia for several moments, his face paling. He slowly shook his head. "I regret, but, much as I admired you—as I still admire you, my lady—it is quite necessary for me to search for a wealthy wife. That is the reason—"

"—The reason that you persuaded a foolish girl to elope with you," she retorted. "And, believe me, it is only the love I have for my stepdaughter which leads me to interfere with your scheme now."

Charlotte made a small dubious noise, but was again silenced by Colin.

"You would have been well served," Sylvia continued, "to find that you had made a second mistake: that I refused to permit Charlotte's money to fall into your hands. I should never be so cruel to her, however, as to allow you to ruin her life. And I am certain you would have ruined it when you discovered that you had married a penniless girl."

"You hate me as much as that?" he asked after a long silence.

"No, Hugo, I do not. It is only that I understand you well enough to know how you would behave if you felt you had been cheated—even though it would have been you who was doing the cheating. I have no doubt that Charlotte will hate you when she learns the truth; but for myself, I do not think you worth the hating."

He recoiled as if she had slapped him, then shaking he bowed. "If you will excuse me, Lady Harmin, I think I shall take my leave of you now." It might be the wisest course, he thought, to do so while the lady was still able to control her companion's anger.

"But not to return to London," Bennett told him. "You might overcome the fury that would be heaped upon you when it was learned how you have deceived everyone with your pretense of being an officer. But I do not think you would be well received there if word were to get around that you had attempted to abduct Lady Charlotte. And despite all our efforts on her behalf to keep the tale quiet, I fear there would be talk."

"She came with me willingly."

"We received a different impression when we arrived. You may as well know, Lannon, that Lady Harmin may have protected you now, but if any word of what has occurred here becomes common gossip, I shall hunt you down and punish you as you so well deserve."

The ferocity in his tone was enough to make the other man take a step backward, fearing an attack. Then, recovering himself, Hugo bowed again and said, "London will not be a welcome place for me, in any case, thanks to my failure in achieving my aim today. I think I shall not see either of you again—at least for some time. However, you may rely upon my discretion."

# CHAPTER
## ❧ 17 ❦

He caught up his hat and left hurriedly, as if still unsure that Sylvia could restrain Bennett's anger, especially after that gentleman's last threat. Watching him leave, Colin exclaimed furiously, "You mean that you are letting him go? With no more than a word? You should have thrashed him—or permitted me to do it."

"That is my feeling as well," Bennett said. "Why did you stop me from doing so?"

"Not for any wish to shelter him," Sylvia was quick to reassure him. "Please believe that I, too, should have liked to see that he was punished. But you must see that my way of handling the affair was the better one. His pride has been deeply hurt, and I believe he will not soon recover from that wound. Also, I feared that, if you should attempt to punish him physically—"

"Attempt? I should most certainly have done so."

"Of course you would have; I did not mean to imply that I have the least doubt of your ability to do so. But I have seen that your wounded shoulder still troubles you at times, although you do what you can to hide the fact. In attacking him, you might have been hurt as well. And that I could not have borne."

Nonetheless, thrilled as he might be by the thought that she had his welfare at heart, Bennett was half-angry with her for her interference at such a time. "It is not the thing for a man to allow a fe—a lady to fight his battles for him."

"No," Colin said, still inflamed at the thought of the villain escaping scot-free, as Hugo's leaving seemed to him. "I should have been the one to do it."

Charlotte murmured a reply, but Sylvia ignored both of them.

"But it *was* my battle," she said to Bennett, her hand upon his arm, as if her touch would impress her words upon him, "as well as yours. More mine, I should think, because it was my stepdaughter who had been endangered. And have you not come to *my* rescue in the past? More than once?"

"That may be, but from what you told the scoundrel just now, you might easily have freed yourself from him merely by telling him the truth about your prospects. He would have bowed out of your life at once."

Sylvia had no doubt Bennett was entirely right about that, but this, rather, was the time for her to recover any ground she had lost by preventing him from fighting Hugo as he had wished to do. "I do not think so. You must remember how furious he was when you came in to rescue me that day. He would have been even more angered to learn the truth then, because he would have blamed me for not informing him sooner that I should be a pauper if I remarried. Now that I know he was not what he pretended, I am the more certain that I was wise to say nothing. As I said just now, I think the man might prove dangerous if he felt he was being deceived in turn. I was most grateful to you for saving me from his anger."

There was much that Bennett wished to say, but the presence of the two younger people prevented him. "We should return to London as soon as we can do so," he said instead.

Sylvia sensed his pent-up feelings and was eager to listen to him. But, like him, she thought it best to wait, so she merely nodded. Disappointed that he would have no opportunity to confront the man who had taken Charlotte away, Colin again urged her from the room, and this time she went meekly.

Taking up Sylvia's cloak and draping it carefully about her shoulders, Bennett said, "We shall talk of this later." There was such tenderness in his tone that Sylvia dared not speak, lest she reveal her own feelings. Still, she felt that he understood as he guided her out of the inn.

By this time, Colin had assisted Charlotte into the carriage, where she huddled in one corner. She had clearly been weeping, despite the young man's attempts to comfort her. When she saw her stepmother, however, her tears stopped, as if Sylvia's presence was enough to dry them, and she sat up, staring into space.

Colin half-rose to allow Sylvia to take his seat, but Charlotte quickly caught his hand, holding him to his place at her side. With a regretful murmur to Sylvia, he sat down once more, and she took the facing seat, Bennett beside her, his hand over hers in the darkness of the carriage. She could not tell the younger man that she much preferred her present position.

The quartet rode in silence until they reached the mansion in Berkeley Square. Still saying nothing, Charlotte allowed Colin to help her down and started quickly for the door, hardly waiting for the footman to open it fully before slipping inside. Pausing only long enough to say a hurried "Thank you" to both gentlemen for their help and suggesting that they use her carriage to return home, Sylvia followed her.

As her stepmother had thought she would do, Charlotte ran up the steps to her bedchamber, but Sylvia was upon her heels and entered the room before she could slam the door. After the waiting servants were dismissed with a nod, Sylvia said, "Charlotte, we must talk."

"I do not wish to talk to you or to anyone," Charlotte said sullenly. "Now, or at any time. And this is *my* room. Please leave me alone."

"I cannot do that."

"Then I shall leave, if you will not."

She turned to the door, but Sylvia was ahead of her, standing in her way.

"Sit down!"

The command was so unlike Sylvia's customary tone that Charlotte obeyed, but her fists were clenched. "I suppose you wish to gloat about the way you have ruined my happiness yet another time. Well, I cannot stop you, but it will do you no good, as I shall not listen."

"You did not sound as if you were particularly happy when we arrived at the inn. I distinctly heard you demanding to be taken home."

"Well . . . I decided . . . I decided that I did not wish a runaway marriage, after all."

"It was a bit late to make such a decision. After all, you *had* run away—"

The girl shrugged, unwilling to allow Sylvia to see

her true feelings. "I had changed my mind about going further, that is all. The idea of an elopement no longer amused me and I preferred to return to London, where I could be married in proper style."

"Ignoring the fact that what you had already done was so improper that it would have ruined your reputation entirely had we not come upon you as we did?"

"I could have made Hugo bring me home." Charlotte's tone was sulky.

"You may have thought at one time that you could make him do as you wished, but I am certain that you now know that is not true. Captain Lannon—I must remember, and so must you, that he was *not* a captain, but an imposter—had doubtless told the innkeeper you were already wed, but of course, the man knew otherwise. You must have gathered something of the kind when he said the man would not permit you to leave until morning."

"You may say that, but—"

"There is no use in your denying it. What I am saying is the truth. You had halted at the sort of low place where the help looks the other way with the payment of a few guineas. You would have been forced to spend the night with Hugo Lannon, whether you wished to do so or not. Then, as he was telling you as we arrived, on the morrow he *would* have brought you back to London, informing me that I would have no choice but to agree to your marriage in order to save you from ruin."

"Well, why should he not put it in those terms, since marriage was what we both wanted?" She spoke with a defiance she was far from feeling. What Sylvia had said to Hugo, and he to her, had come as a shock, revealing as it did that he had not cared for her in the least, but had only wanted her for her fortune. The fact that he had lied about being an officer meant little to her in the face of his other deceit.

If Sylvia and Bennett, and Colin, as well, had overheard their quarrel, *could* she continue to pretend that she had still wanted the marriage? The truth was she had changed her mind about the man long before they reached the low inn at which Hugo had insisted they spend the night. She had wished she were safely back in London . . . and . . . had he truly planned to ruin her if Sylvia did not agree to the marriage?

"Was it?" Sylvia's question broke into her thoughts.

"Yes," she said, untruthfully. "If you and Bennett had not interfered, all would have been well."

"You seemed happy to see us."

"Well, I was not. You had no right to follow me, to interfere with my happiness, as you have done before. As you always wish to do. And why did you have to bring that young Mr. Waite with you and humiliate me before him?"

"That was not my intention, but he was dining with Bennett, so insisted upon accompanying us when he learned you were in trouble."

"I was *not* in trouble. I do not see why you came, any of you."

"Bennett accompanied me," she said after a time, "because I could scarcely make such a journey alone. And *I* came to tell Hugo Lannon that you would have nothing if he insisted upon marrying you. I do not think you remembered to tell him that."

"Why should I have done so? We were not concerned with such matters as money."

"You may not have considered it of importance, but I can assure you that the thought of your fortune weighed heavily with him."

"How can you say that about him?" Charlotte demanded. She knew her stepmother was speaking the truth, but was still loath to own that she had behaved foolishly. It may not have taken her many hours to become disenchanted with the captain, but she would not allow Sylvia to suspect her change of feelings.

"Because, my dear girl—"

"Do not call me that!"

"Very well. But you heard this evening how I had given the *soi disant* captain his *congé* because I had overheard him boasting to his friends that he was about to wed *me* for my fortune."

Charlotte stared at her. "But . . . you said that, I know. But you have no fortune . . . not if you marry."

"That is true, but Hugo did not know that. He thought me a gullible widow, one who could be easily won over by false gallantry. I must own that he flattered me very nicely—I am certain you have learned that he is a master of the art. And if I had been in search of a husband, I think I *might* have considered him."

"You mean—" the girl's disillusionment was complete. "—You mean that his only interest in me was because of my fortune?"

Sylvia nodded, then shook her head. "Not entirely, I should think. Doubtless, he found you a most attractive young lady, one who would grace his house—the house his betrothed must provide him, of course."

"Ohhh!" The girl paced across the room, then threw herself across her bed, sobbing. She had been through an exhausting day, had quickly become disenchanted with the man she thought she had taken away from her stepmother, and above all, felt that she had been humiliated with Colin Waite a witness to everything that happened.

Sylvia sat beside her and gathered her into her arms. "It is nothing so dreadful, after all, my dear. You were mistaken in the man's intentions, but no harm has come of it."

"But what if he . . . if he tells how I . . ."

"There is no need for you to worry about that. You heard Bennett when he warned Hugo that the less said about what has happened, the better it will be for him. In fact, I doubt we shall see Hugo Lannon in London for some time, if ever." She substituted her own clean handkerchief in place of the sodden item Charlotte was twisting between her fingers.

Charlotte looked up at her, biting her lip to stop its trembling before she said, "Then no one need know what I have done, except the three of you?"

"No one at all."

"And Colin . . . Mr. Waite . . . has assured me that no one would think the worse of me. But I am certain they would, if they knew. How kind of Bennett to keep the man silent. But I thought he might have thrashed Hugo to make him promise to say nothing." She sounded half-disappointed that Bennett had not done so.

"No, he would have done, had it been necessary. He wished to do so, as did Colin. But when I told Hugo that he would get no money if you went through with this, it was enough to change his mind about the idea of marriage with you."

Charlotte sobbed louder, her defiance completely overcome by Sylvia's understanding. There was no sign of gloating in her stepmother's attitude toward her, no censure for her foolish behavior. "If only he . . . he keeps his word to be silent."

"I assure you he will do so, my dear. You heard Bennett threaten him if he dares to say anything in the future. And Hugo knows it was not an idle threat."

"Bennett is so good, is he not?"

"Yes, he is." Sylvia's smile was tender as she thought of the unspoken message she had seen in the other's eyes as they left the inn, of his voice when he said, "We shall talk later."

"Did you know that I tried to get him to make love to me?"

He had told her of Charlotte's proposal, of course, when he was so angry at her, but Charlotte need not know of that. It would hurt her further if she thought her friend had been indiscreet about something so important to her. "No," she prevaricated. "He would not speak about something of that sort, you know."

"I know. But he told me that he wished to marry you."

"He did? And he had said nothing to me?" Even now, he had not actually spoken the words. But Sylvia knew that was what he had meant, was it not?

"Well, not in so many words. But I could tell what he had in mind. That was what made me so angry—that he would prefer you to me. That was why I encouraged Hugo. Why I agreed to elope with him."

"Did you think if you eloped with another man it would make Bennett sorry he had refused you?" Sylvia's tone was understanding.

Charlotte hung her head. "I did not think at all. When I thought you were going to be happy with Bennett, I only wanted to get as far away from London, and from you, as I could."

"Yes." Sylvia sighed. "You have always wished to escape from me. But I did not think you would take such extreme measures to do it."

"Not any more. I know now that you only wanted my

good. That is what you have always wanted. But it took *this* to make me understand."

"Then the lesson was not wasted, painful as it has been for all of us. Now, you must get some rest, dear. There are only a few days of the Season left, and you will wish to be able to enjoy them."

Half-asleep, Charlotte permitted Sylvia to help her out of her clothing and into bed. But as Sylvia turned to leave, the girl sat up and flung her arms about her. "You may not be my mama," she said, "but you have done everything for me."

Sylvia returned the hug, the first embrace Charlotte had ever given her. "And I shall continue to do what I can, my dear. When you have found the right young man, I shall be more than happy to permit your marriage. Now, go to sleep and dream of some handsome boy."

She put out the lamp and closed Charlotte's door, then went downstairs, to find Bennett awaiting her. "I sent Colin home, told him to go to bed," he announced. "I thought today's excitement had been enough for the boy."

"It was thoughtful of you to do that. Exactly the sort of consideration for others one would expect of you. But what of yourself, should you not be resting as well? I am concerned about your wound."

"I have told you it is no longer serious. Has not been for some time. And I felt that it was time we talked, that we cleared the air of all the difficulties between us." There was a tenderness in his voice which told her she had been forgiven for what she had done tonight, for all the misunderstandings that had arisen. "Will you truly be a pauper?" he asked. "With no prospects at all?"

"My prospects for the future are quite satisfactory, as long as I remain unwed. Do you not remember how you once taunted that it was important for me to seek a wealthy husband?"

"I said many cruel things to you, I fear. But no one can say that you have angled for a husband of any sort. Do you fear another marriage?"

"N—no. Rather, I should welcome it. To the right man, of course." She was feeling breathless. During the past weeks, she had begun to feel that Bennett had overcome his earlier dislike of her, might even be forming a *tendre* for her. But could she be certain? The gentleman had never said anything . . . Charlotte had said he had told her that he wished—

The expression in his eyes left her in no doubt as he said huskily, "That is what I had hoped."

There was no weakness in his wounded arm, she realized as she was drawn into a close embrace. Then all thought was lost as the magic of his kiss carried her to a paradise she had never known.

# CHAPTER
## ❧ 18 ❧

It was the last ball of the spring Season, and the most elaborate. On the morrow, the Prince Regent would leave London for his summer residence in Brighton, and when his followers trooped in his wake, the Society of the City would be left destitute. Or so nearly so that only a few would think it worth their while to remain longer. They too, would drift away to pay long-neglected summer visits, so that they might tell of their triumphs—real or imagined—to relatives and friends who had stayed at home.

The Countess of Harmin had just concluded a waltz with the gentleman who was her constant companion these past days. As they left the floor, Bennett drew her aside into a small anteroom, taking her in his arms the instant the door had closed behind them.

"You are going to marry me, are you not, my dearest

one?" he asked, prefacing his question with a warm embrace. "And as soon as it can be arranged?"

"Oh, my dear love, that is what I wish to do. More than anything in the world!" As she spoke, Sylvia traced the faint scar beneath his eye, the one he had laughingly owned was not a war wound, but the result of a youthful scuffle. "But you know I cannot; I am not free. Not at present."

"Not free? What entanglements do you have?" he spoke jealously, although her response to his kisses told him that her heart was in his keeping. "Why should there be any reason for delay?"

"I thought this is where we might find you," Charlotte cried, opening the door and entering, Colin at her side. She clicked her tongue in a gesture of censure. "And setting bad examples to your juniors."

"Go away, brat," Bennett ordered, not relaxing his hold about Sylvia.

There was no footstomping this time at the epithet. Instead, the girl only laughed. "In a moment. But first— Sylvia, we shall go to Kent this summer, shall we not?"

"Oh yes," her stepmother said, looking up into Bennett's eyes, "we shall go."

"Then may I tell some friends that they may expect to receive invitations to a house party?"

"Perhaps it would be better to wait before making too many plans. But I suppose it would do no harm to throw out a hint or two."

"That is what I thought." Charlotte turned away, still holding Colin's hand.

The young man looked back. "Might I suggest you try the garden instead? You might find more privacy there." There was laughter in his voice as he led Charlotte toward the dance floor.

"You can see how it is, my dear one. If I delay, it is because of Charlotte. Have you not noticed that since . . . that for the past week, she has turned to me as she has never before done? I can only hope the feeling lasts. She trusts me now, and needs me. I have promised her—"

"Promised her what? Nothing, certainly that could interfere with our happiness."

"N—no, not in time, my dearest one. But I have told her that when she has found the right sort of young man, I shall give her my permission to marry. I must stay with her until then."

He began to laugh. "My foolish darling, have you not seen?"

"Nothing except you."

The avowal won Sylvia another long breathtaking kiss, then he drew her back to a spot behind one of the flowering trees brought in for this occasion and set about the sides of the room to provide just such sheltering alcoves. Drawing aside several branches so that they were able to observe the dancers without drawing attention to themselves, Bennett said, "Look at your charge just now."

The country dance had ended while they had been speaking and partners were now taking their places for another waltz. Charlotte was moving onto the floor on the arm of Colin Waite, who had become her constant companion these past days. The look she bestowed upon the young gentleman when she went into his arms, though perhaps not as rapturous as his own, showed far more interest than had given him in the past.

"You can see for yourself," Bennett said. "All is now well between them."

"True, it does appear that Charlotte does not exactly

take him in aversion. I feared that, after he had accompanied us the night we followed her—"

"Colin handled that in masterly fashion, explaining to her that anyone might mistake the attentions of a philanderer like Lannon and that such a mistake would never count against her in the eyes of those who care for her."

"I am happy that they have become friends, but that does not mean that there is anything more serious than friendship between them."

"True enough, for the present. Although I assure you that it is serious enough on his part. I have listened to his rhapsodizing for hours on end."

"How dreadful for you," she said with a laugh.

"It is, for I would much prefer to talk about you. But at least, her present attitude means that the girl is willing to accept the attention of an honorable young man. But if you fear that she might wander again in the future, only think how much easier it will be if there are two of us in a position to guide her."

"Yes, I had not thought of that."

"Then I suggest you think of it now." He released the branches so that they were screened from the dancers as he drew her once more into his arms.

From the *New York Times* bestselling author
of <u>Forgiving</u> and <u>Bitter Sweet</u>

# LaVyrle Spencer

One of today's best-loved authors of bittersweet
human drama and captivating romance.

| | |
|---|---|
| ___THE ENDEARMENT | 0-515-10396-9/$5.99 |
| ___SPRING FANCY | 0-515-10122-2/$5.99 |
| ___YEARS | 0-515-08489-1/$5.99 |
| ___SEPARATE BEDS | 0-515-09037-9/$5.99 |
| ___HUMMINGBIRD | 0-515-09160-X/$5.50 |
| ___A HEART SPEAKS | 0-515-09039-5/$5.99 |
| ___THE GAMBLE | 0-515-08901-X/$5.99 |
| ___VOWS | 0-515-09477-3/$5.99 |
| ___THE HELLION | 0-515-09951-1/$5.99 |
| ___TWICE LOVED | 0-515-09065-4/$5.99 |
| ___MORNING GLORY | 0-515-10263-6/$5.99 |
| ___BITTER SWEET | 0-515-10521-X/$5.95 |
| ___FORGIVING   (On sale February 1992) | 0-515-10803-0/$5.99 |